CHILDREN'S CLASSICS

# Grimm's Fairy Tales

THE BROTHERS GRIMM

# Grimm's Fairy Tales

PARRAGON

Grimm's Fairy Tales
A Parragon Classic

This edition published in 1994 by
Parragon Book Service Ltd
4 Mulberry Close
Rosslyn Hill, Hampstead
London NW3 5UP

ISBN 1-85813-790-X

Typeset by
Hewer Text Composition Services, Edinburgh
Printed in France by Firmin-Didot Group Hérissey
N° d'impression : 26123

# CONTENTS

# THE TWELVE DANCING PRINCESSES

There was a king who had twelve beautiful daughters. They slept in twelve beds all in one room; and when they went to bed, the doors were shut and locked up; but every morning their shoes were found to be quite worn through as if they had been danced in all night; and yet nobody could find out how it happened, or where they had been.

Then the king made it known to all the land, that if any person could discover the secret, and find out where it was that the princesses danced in the night, he should have the one he liked best for his wife, and should be king after his death; but whoever tried and did not succeed, after three days and nights, should be put to death.

A king's son soon came. He was well entertained, and in the evening was taken to the chamber next to the one where the princesses lay in their twelve beds. There he was to sit and watch where they went to dance; and, in order that nothing might pass without his hearing it, the door of his chamber was left open. But the king's son soon fell asleep; and when he awoke in the morning he found that the princesses had all been dancing, for the soles of their shoes were full of holes. The same thing happened the second and third night: so the king ordered his head to be cut off. After him came several others; but they had all the same luck, and all lost their lives in the same manner.

Now it chanced that an old soldier, who had been wounded in battle and could fight no longer, passed through the country where this king reigned: and as he was travelling through a wood, he met an old woman, who asked him where he was going. "I hardly know where I am going, or what I had better do," said the soldier; "but I think I should like very well to find out where it is that the princesses dance, and then in time I might be a king." "Well," said the old dame, "that is no very hard task: only take care not to drink any of the wine which one of the princesses will bring to you in the evening; and as soon as she leaves you pretend to be fast asleep."

Then she gave him a cloak, and said, "As soon as you put that on you will become invisible, and you will then be able to follow the princesses wherever they go." When the soldier heard all this good counsel, he determined to try his luck: so he went to the king, and said he was willing to undertake the task.

He was as well received as the others had been, and the king ordered fine royal robes to be given him; and when the evening came he was led to the outer chamber. Just as he was going to lie down, the eldest of the princesses brought him a cup of wine; but the soldier threw it all away secretly, taking care not to drink a drop. Then he laid himself down on his bed, and in a little while began to snore very loud as if he was fast asleep. When the twelve princesses heard this they laughed heartily; and the eldest said, "This fellow too might have done a wiser thing than lose his life in this way!" Then they rose up and opened their drawers and boxes, and took out all their fine clothes, and dressed themselves at the glass, and skipped about as if they were eager to begin dancing. But the youngest said, "I don't know how it is, while you are so happy I feel very uneasy; I am sure some mischance will befall us." "You simpleton," said the eldest, "you are always afraid; have you forgotten how many kings' sons have already watched us in vain? And as for this soldier, even if I had not given him his sleeping draught, he would have slept soundly enough."

When they were all ready, they went and looked at the soldier; but he snored on, and did not stir hand or foot: so they thought they were quite safe; and the eldest went up to her own bed and clapped her hands, and the bed sunk into the floor and a trap-door flew open. The soldier saw them going down through the trap-door one after another, the eldest leading the way; and thinking he had no time to lose, he jumped up, put on the cloak which the old woman had given him, and followed them; but in the middle of the stairs he trod on the gown of the youngest princess, and she cried out to her sisters, "All is not right; some one took hold of my gown." "You silly creature!" said the eldest, "it is nothing but a nail in the wall." Then down they all went, and at the bottom they found themselves in a most delightful grove of trees; and the leaves were all of silver, and glittered and sparkled beautifully. The soldier wished to take away some token of the place; so he broke off a little branch, and there came a loud noise from the tree. Then the youngest daughter said again, "I am sure all is not right—did not you hear that noise? That never happened before." But the eldest said, "It is only our princes, who are shouting for joy at our approach."

Then they came to another grove of trees, where all

3

the leaves were of gold; and afterwards to a third, where the leaves were all glittering diamonds. And the soldier broke a branch from each; and every time there was a loud noise, which made the youngest sister tremble with fear; but the eldest still said, It was only the princes, who were crying for joy. So they went on till they came to a great lake; and at the side of the lake there lay twelve little boats with twelve handsome princes in them, who seemed to be waiting there for the princesses.

One of the princesses went into each boat, and the soldier stepped into the same boat with the youngest. As they were rowing over the lake, the prince who was in the boat with the youngest princess and the soldier said, "I do not know why it is, but though I am rowing with all my might we do not get on so fast as usual, and I am quite tired: the boat seems very heavy to-day." "It is only the heat of the weather," said the princess; "I feel it very warm too."

On the other side of the lake stood a fine illuminated castle, from which came the merry music of horns and trumpets. There they all landed, and went into the castle, and each prince danced with his princess; and the soldier, who was all the time invisible, danced with them too; and when any of the princesses had a cup of wine set by her, he drank it all up, so that when she put the cup to her mouth it was empty. At this, too, the youngest sister was terribly frightened, but the eldest always silenced her. They danced on till three o'clock in the morning, and then all their shoes were worn out, so that they were obliged to leave off. The princes rowed them back again over the lake; (but this time the soldier placed himself in the boat with the eldest princess;) and on the opposite shore they took leave of each other, the princesses promising to come again the next night.

When they came to the stairs, the soldier ran on before the princesses, and laid himself down; and as the twelve sisters slowly came up very much tired, they heard him snoring in his bed; so they said, "Now all is quite safe;" then they undressed themselves, put away their fine clothes, pulled off their shoes, and went to bed. In the morning the soldier said nothing about what had happened, but determined to see more of this strange adventure, and went again the second and third night; and every thing happened just as before; the princesses danced each time till their shoes were worn to pieces, and then returned home. However, on the third night the soldier carried away one of the golden cups as a token of where he had been.

As soon as the time came when he was to declare the secret, he was taken before the king with the three branches and the golden cup; and the twelve princesses stood listening behind the door to hear what he would say. And when the king asked him. "Where do my twelve daughters dance at night?" he answered, "With twelve princes in a castle under ground." And then he told the king all that had happened, and showed him the three branches and the golden cup which he had brought with him. Then the king called for the princesses, and asked them whether what the soldier said was true: and when they saw that they were discovered, and that it was of no use to deny what had happened, they confessed it all. And the king asked the soldier which of them he would choose for his wife; and he answered, "I am not very young, so I will have the eldest."—And they were married that very day, and the soldier was chosen to be the king's heir.

# TOM THUMB

There was once a poor woodman sitting by the fire in his cottage, and his wife sat by his side spinning. "How lonely it is," said he, "for you and me to sit here by ourselves without any children to play about and amuse us, while other people seem so happy and merry with their children!" "What you say is very true," said the wife, sighing and turning round her wheel, "how happy should I be if I had but one child! and if it were ever so small, nay, if it were no bigger than my thumb, I should be very happy, and love it dearly." Now it came to pass that this good woman's wish was fulfilled just as she desired; for, some time afterwards, she had a little boy who was quite healthy and strong, but not much bigger than my thumb. So they said, "Well, we cannot say we have not got what we wished for, and, little as he is, we all love him dearly;" and they called him Tom Thumb.

They gave him plenty of food, yet he never grew bigger, but remained just the same size as when he was born; still his eyes were sharp and sparkling, and he soon showed himself to be a clever little fellow, who always knew well what he was about. One day, as the woodman was getting ready to go into the wood to cut fuel, he said, "I wish I had some one to bring the cart after me, for I want to make haste." "O father!" cried Tom, "I will take care of that; the cart shall be in the wood by the time you want it." Then the woodman laughed, and said, "How can that be? you cannot reach up to the horse's bridle." "Never mind that, father," said Tom; "if my mother will only harness the horse, I will get into his ear and tell him which way to go." "Well," said the father, "we will try for once."

When the time came, the mother harnessed the horse to the cart, and put Tom into his ear; and as he sat there, the little man told the beast how to go, crying out, "Go on," and "Stop," as he wanted; so the horse went on just as if the woodman had driven it himself into the wood. It happened that, as the horse was going a little too fast, and Tom was calling out "Gently! gently!" two strangers came up. "What an odd thing that is!" said one, "there is a cart going along and I hear a carter talking to the horse, but can see no one." "That is strange," said the other; "let us follow the cart and see where it goes." So they went on into the wood, till at last they came to the place where the woodman was. Then Tom Thumb, seeing his father, cried out, "See, father, here I am, with the cart, all right and safe; now take me down." So his father took hold of the horse with one hand, and with the other took his son out of the ear; then he put him down upon a straw, where he sat as merry as you please. The two strangers were all this time looking on, and did not know what to say for wonder. At last one took the other aside and said, "That little urchin will make our fortune if we can get him and carry him about from town to town as a show: we must buy him." So they went to the woodman and asked him what he would take for the little man: "He will be better off," said they, "with us than with you." "I won't sell him at all," said the father, "my own flesh and blood is dearer to me than all the silver and gold in the world." But Tom, hearing of the bargain they wanted to make, crept up his father's coat to his shoulder, and whispered in his ear, "Take the money, father, and let them have me, I'll soon come back to you."

So the woodman at last agreed to sell Tom to the strangers for a large piece of gold. "Where do you like to sit?" said one of them. "Oh! put me on the rim of your hat, that will be a nice gallery for me; I can walk about there, and see the country as we go along." So they did as he wished; and when Tom had taken leave of his father, they took him away with them. They journeyed on till it began to be dusky, and then the little man said, "Let me get down, I'm tired." So the man took off his hat and set him down on a clod of earth in a ploughed field by the side of the road. But Tom ran about amongst the furrows, and at last slipt into an old mouse-hole. "Good night, masters," said he, "I'm off! mind and look sharp after me the next time." They ran directly to the place, and poked the ends of their sticks into the mouse-hole, but all in vain; Tom only crawled farther and farther in, and at last it became quite dark, so that they were obliged to go their way without their prize, as sulky as you please.

When Tom found they were gone, he came out of his hiding-place. "What dangerous walking it is," said he, "in this ploughed field! If I were to fall from one of these great clods, I should certainly break my neck." At last, by good luck, he found a large empty snail-shell. "This is lucky," said he, "I can sleep here very well," and in he crept. Just as he was falling asleep he heard two men passing, and one said to the other, "How shall we manage to steal that rich parson's silver and gold?" "I'll

8

tell you," cried Tom. "What noise was that?" said the thief, frightened, "I am sure I heard some one speak." They stood still listening, and Tom said, "Take me with you, and I'll soon show you how to get the parson's money." "But where are you?" said they. "Look about on the ground," answered he, "and listen where the sound comes from." At last the thieves found him out, and lifted him up in their hands. "You little urchin!" said they, "what can you do for us?" "Why I can get between the iron window-bars of the parson's house, and throw you out whatever you want." "That's a good thought," said the thieves, "come along, we shall see what you can do."

When they came to the parson's house, Tom slipt through the window-bars into the room, and then called out as loud as he could bawl, "Will you have all that is here?" At this the thieves were frightened, and said, "Softly, softly! Speak low, that you may not awaken any body." But Tom pretended not to understand them, and bawled out again, "How much will you have? Shall I throw it all out?" Now the cook lay in the next room, and hearing a noise she raised herself in her bed and listened. Meantime the thieves were frightened, and ran off to a little distance; but at last they plucked up courage, and said, "The little urchin is only trying to make fools of us." So they came back and whispered softly to him, saying, "Now let us have no more of your jokes, but throw out some of the money." Then Tom called out as loud as he could, "Very well: hold your hands, here it comes." The cook heard this quite plain, so she sprang out of bed and ran to open the door. The thieves ran off as if a wolf was at their tails; and the maid, having groped about and found nothing, went away for a light. By the time she returned, Tom had slipt off into the barn; and when the cook had looked about and searched every hole and corner, and found nobody, she went to bed, thinking she must have been dreaming with her eyes open. The little man crawled about in the hay-loft, and at last found a glorious place to finish his night's rest in; so he laid himself down, meaning to sleep till day-light, and then find his way home to his father and mother. But, alas! how cruelly was he disappointed! what crosses and sorrows happen in this world! The cook got up early before day-break to feed the cows: she went straight to the hay-loft, and carried away a large bundle of hay with the little man in the middle of it fast asleep. He still, however, slept on, and did not awake till he found himself in the mouth of the cow, who had taken him up with a mouthful of hay: "Good lack-a-day!" said he, "how did I manage to tumble into the mill?" But he soon found out where he really was, and was obliged to have all his wits about him in order that he might not get between the cow's teeth, and so be crushed to death. At last down he went into her stomach. "It is rather dark here," said he; "they forgot to build windows in this room to let the sun in: a candle would be no bad thing."

Though he made the best of his bad luck, he did not like his quarters at all; and the worst of it was, that more and more hay was always coming down, and the space in which he was became smaller and smaller. At last he cried out as loud as he could, "Don't bring me any more hay! Don't bring me any more hay!" The maid happened to be just then milking the cow, and hearing some one speak and seeing nobody, and yet being quite sure it was the same voice that she had heard in the night,

10

she was so frightened that she fell off her stool and overset the milk-pail. She ran off as fast as she could to her master the parson, and said, "Sir, sir, the cow is talking!" But the parson said, "Woman, thou art surely mad!" However, he went with her into the cow-house to see what was the matter. Scarcely had they set their foot on the threshold, when Tom called out, "Don't bring me any more hay!" Then the parson himself was frightened; and thinking the cow was surely bewitched, ordered that she should be killed directly. So the cow was killed, and the stomach, in which Tom lay, was thrown out upon a dunghill.

Tom soon set himself to work to get out, which was not a very easy task; but at last, just as he had made room to get his head out, a new misfortune befell him: a hungry wolf sprang out, and swallowed the whole stomach with Tom in it at a single gulp, and ran away. Tom, however, was not disheartened; and, thinking the wolf would not dislike having some chat with him as he was going along, he called out, "My good friend, I can show you a famous treat." "Where's that?" said the wolf. "In such and such a house," said Tom, describing his father's house, "you can crawl through the drain into the kitchen, and there you will find cakes, ham, beef, and every thing your heart can desire." The wolf did not want to be asked twice; so that very night he went to the house and crawled through the drain into the kitchen, and ate and drank there to his heart's content. As soon as he was satisfied, he wanted to get away, but he had eaten so much that he could not get out the same way that he came in. This was just what Tom had reckoned upon; and he now began to set up a great shout, making all the noise he could. "Will you be quiet?" said the wolf:

"you'll awaken every body in the house." "What's that to me?" said the little man: "you have had your frolic, now I've a mind to be merry myself;" and he began again singing and shouting as loud as he could.

The woodman and his wife, being awakened by the noise, peeped through a crack in the door; but when they saw that the wolf was there, you may well suppose that they were terribly frightened; and the woodman ran for his axe, and gave his wife a scythe.—"Now do you stay behind," said the woodman; "and when I have knocked him on the head, do you rip up his belly for him with the scythe." Tom heard all this, and said, "Father, father! I am here, the wolf has swallowed me:" and his father said, "Heaven be praised! we have found our dear child again;" and he told his wife not to use the scythe, for fear she should hurt him. Then he aimed a great blow, and struck the wolf on the head, and killed him on the spot; and when he was dead they cut open his body and set Tommy free. "Ah!" said the father, "what fears we have had for you!" "Yes, father," answered he, "I have travelled all over the world, since we parted, in one way or other; and now I am very glad to get fresh air again." "Why, where have you been?" said his father. "I have been in a mouse-hole, in a snail-shell, down a cow's throat, and in the wolf's belly; and yet here I am again safe and sound." "Well," said they "we will not sell you again for all the riches in the world." So they hugged and kissed their dear little son, and gave him plenty to eat and drink, and fetched new clothes for him, for his old ones were quite spoiled on his journey.

# KING GRISLY-BEARD

A great king had a daughter who was very beautiful, but so proud and haughty and conceited, that none of the princes who came to ask her in marriage were good enough for her, and she only made sport of them.

Once upon a time the king held a great feast, and invited all her suitors; and they sat in a row according to their rank, kings and princes and dukes and earls. Then the princess came in and passed by them all, but she had something spiteful to say to every one. The first was too fat: "He's as round as a tub," said she. The next was too tall: "What a maypole!" said she. The next was too short: "What a dumpling!" said she. The fourth was too pale, and she called him "Wallface." The fifth was too red, so she called him "Cockscomb." The sixth was not straight enough, so she said he was like a green stick that had been laid to dry over a baker's oven. And thus she had some joke to crack upon every one: but she laughed more than all at a good king who was there. "Look at him," said she, "his beard is like an old mop, he shall be called Grisly-beard." So the king got the nickname of Grisly-beard.

But the old king was very angry when he saw how his daughter behaved, and how she ill-treated all his guests; and he vowed that, willing or unwilling, she should marry the first beggar that came to the door.

Two days after there came by a travelling musician, who began to sing under the window, and beg alms: and when the king heard him, he said, "Let him come in." So they brought in a dirty-looking fellow; and when he had sung before the king and the princess, he begged a boon. Then the king said, "You have sung so well, that I will give you my daughter for your wife." The princess begged and prayed; but the king said, "I have sworn to give you to the first beggar, and I will keep my word." So words and tears were of no avail; the parson was sent for, and she was married to the musician. When this was over, the king said, "Now get ready to go; you must not stay here; you must travel on with your husband."

Then the beggar departed, and took her with him; and they soon came to a great wood. "Pray," said she, "whose is this wood?" "It belongs to king Grisly-beard," answered he; "hadst thou taken him, all had been thine." "Ah! unlucky wretch that I am!" sighed she, "would that I had married king Grisly-beard!" Next they came to some fine meadows. "Whose are these beautiful green meadows?" said she. "They belong to king Grisly-beard; hadst thou taken him, they had all been thine." "Ah! unlucky wretch that I am!" said she, "would that I had married king Grisly-beard!"

Then they came to a great city. "Whose is this noble city?" said she. "It belongs to king Grisly-beard; hadst thou taken him, it had all been thine." "Ah! miserable wretch that I am!" sighed she, "why did I not marry king Grisly-beard?" "That is no business of mine," said the musician; "why should you wish for another husband? am not I good enough for you?"

At last they came to a small cottage. "What a paltry place!" said she; "to whom does that little dirty hole belong?" The musician answered, "That is your and my house, where we are to live." "Where are your servants?" cried she. "What do we want with servants?"

said he, "you must do for yourself whatever is to be done. Now make the fire, and put on water and cook my supper, for I am very tired." But the princess knew nothing of making fires and cooking, and the beggar was forced to help her. When they had eaten a very scanty meal they went to bed; but the musician called her up very early in the morning to clean the house. Thus they lived for two days: and when they had eaten up all there was in the cottage, the man said, "Wife, we can't go on thus, spending money and earning nothing. You must learn to weave baskets." Then he went out and cut willows and brought them home, and she began to weave: but it made her fingers very sore. "I see this work won't do," said he, "try and spin; perhaps you will do that better." So she sat down and tried to spin; but the threads cut her tender fingers till the blood ran. "See now," said the musician, "you are good for nothing, you can do no work;—what a bargain I have got! However, I'll try and set up a trade in pots and pans, and you shall stand in the market and sell them." "Alas!" sighed she, "when I stand in the market and any of my father's court pass by and see me there, how they will laugh at me!"

But the beggar did not care for that; and said she must work, if she did not wish to die of hunger. At first the trade went well; for many people, seeing such a beautiful woman, went to buy her wares, and paid their money without thinking of taking away the goods. They lived on this as long as it lasted, and then her husband bought a fresh lot of ware, and she sat herself down with it in a corner of the market; but a drunken soldier soon came by, and rode his horse against her stall and broke all her goods into a thousand pieces. Then she began to weep, and knew not what to do. "Ah! what will become of me!" said she; "what will my husband say?" So she ran home and told him all. "Who would have thought you would have been so silly," said he, "as to put an earthenware stall in the corner of the market, where every body passes?—But let us have no more crying; I see you are not fit for this sort of work: so I have been to the king's palace, and asked if they did not want a kitchen-maid, and they have promised to take you, and there you will have plenty to eat."

Thus the princess became a kitchen-maid, and helped the cook to do all the dirtiest work: she was allowed to carry home some of the meat that was left, and on this she and her husband lived.

She had not been there long, before she heard that the king's eldest son was passing by, going to be married, and she went to one of the windows and looked out. Every thing was ready, and all the pomp and splendour of the court was there. Then she thought with an aching heart on her own sad fate, and bitterly grieved for the pride and folly which had brought her so low. And the servants gave her some of the rich meats, which she put into her basket to take home.

All on a sudden, as she was going out, in came the king's son in golden clothes: and when he saw a beautiful woman at the door, he took her by the hand, and said she should be his partner in the dance: but she trembled for fear, for she saw that it was king Grisly-beard, who was making sport of her. However, he kept fast hold and led her in; and the cover of the basket came off, so that the meats in it fell all about. Then every body laughed and jeered at her; and she was so abashed that she wished herself a thousand feet deep in

16

the earth. She sprang to the door to run away; but on the steps king Grisly-beard overtook and brought her back, and said, "Fear me not! I am the musician who has lived with you in the hut: I brought you there because I loved you. I am also the soldier who overset your stall. I have done all this only to cure you of pride, and to punish you for the ill-treatment you bestowed on me. Now all is over; you have learnt wisdom, your faults are gone, and it is time to celebrate our marriage feast!"

Then the chamberlains came and brought her the most beautiful robes: and her father and his whole court were there already, and congratulated her on her marriage. Joy was in every face. The feast was grand, and all were merry; and I wish you and I had been of the party.

# THE ELVES AND THE SHOEMAKER

There was once a shoemaker who worked very hard and was very honest; but still he could not earn enough to live upon, and at last all he had in the world was gone, except just leather enough to make one pair of shoes. Then he cut them all ready to make up the next day, meaning to get up early in the morning to work. His conscience was clear and his heart light amidst all his troubles; so he went peaceably to bed, left all his cares to heaven, and fell asleep. In the morning, after he had said his prayers, he set himself down to his work, when, to his great wonder, there stood the shoes, all ready made, upon the table. The good man knew not what to say or think of this strange event. He looked at the workmanship; there was not one false stitch in the whole job; and all was so neat and true, that it was a complete masterpiece.

That same day a customer came in, and the shoes pleased him so well that he willingly paid a price higher than usual for them; and the poor shoemaker with the money bought leather enough to make two pairs more. In the evening he cut out the work, and went to bed early that he might get up and begin betimes next day: but he was saved all the trouble, for when he got up in the morning the work was finished ready to his hand. Presently in came buyers, who paid him handsomely for his goods, so that he bought leather enough for four pairs more. He cut out the work again over night, and found it finished in the morning as before; and so it went on for some time: what was got ready in the evening was always done by daybreak, and the good man soon became thriving and prosperous again.

One evening about Christmas time, as he and his wife were sitting over the fire chatting together, he said to her, "I should like to sit up and watch to-night, that we may see who it is that comes and does my work for me." The wife liked the thought; so they left a light burning, and hid themselves in the corner of the room behind a curtain that was hung up there, and watched what should happen.

As soon as it was midnight, there came two little naked dwarfs; and they sat themselves upon the shoemaker's bench, took up all the work that was cut out, and began to ply with their little fingers, stitching and rapping and tapping away at such a rate, that the shoemaker was all amazement, and could not take his eyes off for a moment. And on they went till the job was quite finished, and the shoes stood ready for use upon the table. This was long before daybreak; and then they bustled away as quick as lightning.

The next day the wife said to the shoemaker, "These little wights have made us rich, and we ought to be thankful to them, and do them a good office in return. I am quite vexed to see them run about as they do; they have nothing upon their backs to keep off the cold. I'll tell you what, I will make each of them a shirt, and a coat and waistcoat, and a pair of pantaloons into the bargain; do you make each of them a little pair of shoes."

The thought pleased the good shoemaker very much; and one evening, when all the things were ready, they laid them on the table instead of the work that they used to cut out, and then went and hid themselves to watch what the little elves would do. About midnight they came in, and were going to sit down to their work as usual; but when they saw the clothes lying for them, they laughed and were greatly delighted. Then they dressed themselves in the twinkling of an eye, and danced and capered and sprang about as merry as could be, till at last they danced out at the door over the green; and the shoemaker saw them no more: but every thing went well with him from that time forward, as long as he lived.

# THE KING OF
# THE GOLDEN MOUNTAIN

A certain merchant had two children, a son and daughter, both very young, and scarcely able to run alone. He had two richly laden ships then making a voyage upon the seas, in which he had embarked all his property, in the hope of making great gains, when the news came that they were lost. Thus from being a rich man he became very poor, so that nothing was left him but one small plot of land; and, to relieve his mind a little of his trouble, he often went out to walk there.

One day, as he was roving along, a little rough-looking dwarf stood before him, and asked him why he was so sorrowful, and what it was that he took so deeply to heart. But the merchant replied, "If you could do me any good, I would tell you." "Who knows but I may?" said the little man; "tell me what is the matter, and perhaps I can be of some service." Then the merchant told him how all his wealth was gone to the bottom of the sea, and how he had nothing left except that little plot of land. "Oh! trouble not yourself about that," said the dwarf; "only promise to bring me here, twelve years hence, whatever meets you first on your return home, and I will give you as much gold as you please." The merchant thought this was no great request; that it would most likely be his dog, or something of that sort, but forgot his little child: so he agreed to the bargain, and signed and sealed the engagement to do what was required.

But as he drew near home, his little boy was so pleased to see him, that he crept behind him and laid fast hold of his legs. Then the father started with fear, and saw what it was that he had bound himself to do; but as no gold was come, he consoled himself by thinking that it was only a joke that the dwarf was playing him.

About a month afterwards he went up stairs into an old lumber room to look for some old iron, that he might sell it and raise a little money; and there he saw a large pile of gold lying on the floor. At the sight of this he was greatly delighted, went into trade again, and became a greater merchant than before.

Meantime his son grew up, and as the end of the twelve years drew near, the merchant became very anxious and thoughtful; so that care and sorrow were written upon his face. The son one day asked what was the matter: but his father refused to tell for some time; at last however he said that he had, without knowing it, sold him to a little ugly-looking dwarf for a great quantity of gold; and that the twelve years were coming round when he must perform his agreement. Then the son said, "Father, give yourself very little trouble about that; depend upon it I shall be too much for the little man."

When the time came, they went out together to the appointed place; and the son drew a circle on the ground, and set himself and his father in the middle. The little dwarf soon came, and said to the merchant, "Have you brought me what you promised?" The old man was silent, but his son answered, "What do you want here?" The dwarf said, "I come to talk with your father, not with you" "You have deceived and betrayed my father," said the son; "give him up his bond." "No,"

21

replied the other, "I will not yield up my rights." Upon this a long dispute arose; and at last it was agreed that the son should be put into an open boat, that lay on the side of a piece of water hard by, and that the father should push him off with his own hand; so that he should be turned adrift. Then he took leave of his father, and set himself in the boat; and as it was pushed off it heaved, and fell on one side into the water: so the merchant thought that his son was lost, and went home very sorrowful.

But the boat went safely on, and did not sink; and the young man sat securely within, till at length it ran ashore upon an unknown land. As he jumped upon the shore, he saw before him a beautiful castle, but empty and desolate within, for it was enchanted. At last, however, he found a white snake in one of the chambers.

Now the white snake was an enchanted princess; and she rejoiced greatly to see him, and said, "Art thou at last come to be my deliverer? Twelve long years have I waited for thee, for thou alone canst save me. This night twelve men will come: their faces will be black, and they will be hung round with chains. They will ask what thou dost here; but be silent, give no answer, and let them do what they will—beat and torment thee. Suffer all, only speak not a word, and at twelve o'clock they must depart. The second night twelve others will come; and the third night twenty-four, who will even cut off thy head; but at the twelfth hour of that night their power is gone, and I shall be free, and will come and bring thee the water of life and health." And all came to pass as she had said; the merchant's son spoke not a word, and the third night the princess appeared, and fell on his neck and kissed him; joy and gladness burst forth throughout the castle; the wedding was celebrated, and he was king of the Golden Mountain.

They lived together very happily, and the queen had a son. Eight years had passed over their heads when the king thought of his father: and his heart was moved, and he longed to see him once again. But the queen opposed his going, and said, "I know well that misfortunes will come." However, he gave her no rest till she consented. At his departure she presented him with a wishing-ring, and said, "Take this ring, and put it on your finger; whatever you wish it will bring you: only promise that you will not make use of it to bring me hence to your father's." Then he promised what she asked, and put the ring on his finger, and wished himself near the town where his father lived. He found himself at the gates in a moment; but the guards would not let him enter, because he was so strangely clad. So he went up to a neighbouring mountain where a shepherd dwelt, and borrowed his old frock, and thus passed unobserved into the town. When he came to his father's house, he said he was his son; but the merchant would not believe him, and said he had had but one son, who he knew was long since dead; and as he was only dressed like a poor shepherd, he would not even offer him any thing to eat. The king however persisted that he was his son, and said, "Is there no mark by which you would know if I am really your son?" "Yes," observed his mother, "our son has a mark like a raspberry under the right arm." Then he showed them the mark, and they were satisfied that what he had said was true. He next told them how he was king of the Golden Mountain, and was married to a princess, and had a son seven years old. But the merchant said, "That can never be true; he must be a fine king truly who travels about in a shepherd's frock." At this the son was very angry; and, forgetting his promise, turned his ring, and wished for his queen and son. In an instant they stood before him; but the queen wept, and said he had broken his word, and misfortune would follow. He did all he could to soothe her, and she at last appeared to be appeased; but she was not so in reality, and only meditated how she should take her revenge.

One day he took her to walk with him out of the town, and showed her the spot where the boat was turned adrift upon the wide waters. Then he sat himself down, and said, "I am very much tired; sit by me, I will rest my head in your lap, and sleep a while." As soon as he had fallen asleep, however, she drew the ring from his finger, and crept softly away, and wished herself and her son at home in their kingdom. And when the king awoke, he found himself alone, and saw that the ring was gone from his finger. "I can never return to my father's house," said he; "they would say I am a sorcerer; I will journey forth into the world till I come again to my kingdom."

So saying, he set out and travelled till he came to a mountain, where three giants were sharing their inheritance; and as they saw him pass, they cried out and said, "Little men have sharp wits; he shall divide the inheritance between us." Now it consisted of a sword that cut off an enemy's head whenever the wearer gave the words "Heads off!"—a cloak that made the owner invisible, or gave him any form he pleased; and a pair of boots that transported the person who put them on wherever he wished. The king said they must

24

first let him try these wonderful things, that he might know how to set a value upon them. Then they gave him the cloak, and he wished himself a fly, and in a moment he was a fly. "The cloak is very well," said he; "now give me the sword." "No," said they, "not unless you promise not to say 'Heads off!' for if you do, we are all dead men." So they gave it him on condition that he tried its virtue only on a tree. He next asked for the boots also; and the moment he had all three in his possession he wished himself at the Golden Mountain; and there he was in an instant. So the giants were left behind with no inheritance to divide or quarrel about.

As he came near to the castle he heard the sound of merry music; and the people around told him that his queen was about to celebrate her marriage with another prince. Then he threw his cloak around him, and passed through the castle, and placed himself by the side of his queen, where no one saw him. But when any thing to eat was put upon her plate, he took it away and ate it himself; and when a glass of wine was handed to her, he took and drank it: and thus, though they kept on serving her with meat and drink, her plate continued always empty.

Upon this, fear and remorse came over her, and she went into her chamber and wept; and he followed her there. "Alas!" said she to herself, "did not my deliverer come? why then doth enchantment still surround me?"

"Thou traitress!" said he, "thy deliverer indeed came, and now is near thee: has he deserved this of thee?" And he went out and dismissed the company, and said the wedding was at an end, for that he was returned to his kingdom: but the princes and nobles and counsellors mocked at him. However, he would enter into no parley with them, but only demanded whether they would depart in peace, or not. Then they turned and tried to seize him; but he drew his sword, and, with a word, the traitors' heads fell before him; and he was once more king of the Golden Mountain.

# THE GOLDEN GOOSE

There was a man who had three sons. The youngest was called Dummling, and was on all occasions despised and ill-treated by the whole family. It happened that the eldest took it into his head one day to go into the wood to cut fuel; and his mother gave him a delicious pasty and a bottle of wine to take with him, that he might refresh himself at his work. As he went into the wood, a little old man bid him good day, and said, "Give me a little piece of meat from your plate, and a little wine out of your bottle; I am very hungry and thirsty." But this clever young man said, "Give you my meat and wine! No, I thank you; I should not have enough left for myself:" and away he went. He soon began to cut down a tree; but he had not worked long before he missed his stroke, and cut himself, and was obliged to go home to have the wound dressed. Now it was the little old man that caused him this mischief.

Next went out the second son to work; and his mother gave him too a pasty and a bottle of wine. And the same little old man met him also, and asked him for something to eat and drink. But he too thought himself vastly clever, and said, "Whatever you get, I shall lose;

26

so go your way!" The little man took care that he should
have his reward; and the second stroke that he aimed
against a tree, hit him on the leg; so that he too was
forced to go home.

Then Dummling said, "Father, I should like to go
and cut wood too." But his father answered, "Your
brothers have both lamed themselves; you had better
stay at home, for you know nothing of the business."
But Dummling was very pressing; and at last his father
said, "Go your way; you will be wiser when you have
suffered for your folly." And his mother gave him only
some dry bread, and a bottle of sour beer; but when he
went into the wood, he met the little old man, who said,
"Give me some meat and drink, for I am very hungry
and thirsty." Dummling said, "I have only dry bread
and sour beer; if that will suit you, we will sit down
and eat it together." So they sat down; and when the
lad pulled out his bread, behold it was turned into a
capital pasty, and his sour beer became delightful wine.
They ate and drank heartily; and when they had done,
the little man said, "As you have a kind heart, and have
been willing to share every thing with me, I will send
a blessing upon you. There stands an old tree; cut it
down, and you will find something at the root." Then
he took his leave, and went his way.

Dummling set to work, and cut down the tree; and
when it fell, he found in a hollow under the roots a
goose with feathers of pure gold. He took it up, and
went on to an inn, where he proposed to sleep for the
night. The landlord had three daughters; and when they
saw the goose, they were very curious to examine what
this wonderful bird could be, and wished very much
to pluck one of the feathers out of its tail. At last the

27

eldest said, "I must and will have a feather." So she waited till his back was turned, and then seized the goose by the wing; but to her great surprise there she stuck, for neither hand nor finger could she get away again. Presently in came the second sister, and thought to have a feather too; but the moment she touched her sister, there she too hung fast. At last came the third, and wanted a feather; but the other two cried out, "Keep away! for heaven's sake, keep away!" However, she did not understand what they meant. "If they are there," thought she, "I may as well be there too." So she went up to them; but the moment she touched her sisters she stuck fast, and hung to the goose as they did. And so they kept company with the goose all night.

The next morning Dummling carried off the goose under his arm; and took no notice of the three girls, but went out with them sticking fast behind; and wherever he travelled, they too were obliged to follow, whether they would or no, as fast as their legs could carry them.

In the middle of a field the parson met them; and when he saw the train, he said, "Are you not ashamed of yourselves, you bold girls, to run after the young man in that way over the fields? is that proper behaviour?" Then he took the youngest by the hand to lead her away; but the moment he touched her he too hung fast, and followed in the train. Presently up came the clerk; and when he saw his master the parson running after the three girls, he wondered greatly, and said, "Hollo! hollo! your reverence! whither so fast? there is a christening to-day." Then he ran up, and took him by the gown, and in a moment he was fast too. As the five were thus trudging along, one behind another, they met two labourers with their mattocks coming from work; and the parson cried out to them to set him free. But scarcely had they touched him, when they too fell into the ranks, and so made seven, all running after Dummling and his goose.

At last they arrived at a city, where reigned a king who had an only daughter. The princess was of so thoughtful and serious a turn of mind that no one could make her laugh; and the king had proclaimed to all the world, that whoever could make her laugh should have her for his wife. When the young man heard this, he went to her with his goose and all its train; and as soon as she saw the seven all hanging together, and running about, treading on each other's heels she could not help bursting into a long and loud laugh. Then Dummling claimed her for his wife; the wedding was celebrated, and he was heir to the kingdom, and lived long and happily with his wife.

## HANSEL AND GRETTEL

Hansel one day took his sister Grettel by the hand, and said, "Since our poor mother died we have had no happy days; for our new mother beats us all day long and when we go near her, she pushes us away. We have nothing but hard crusts to eat; and the little dog that lies by the fire is better off than we; for he sometimes has a nice piece of meat thrown to him. Heaven have mercy upon us! O if our poor mother knew how we are used! Come, we will go and travel over the wide world.' They went the whole day walking over the fields, till in the

29

evening they came to a great wood; and then they were so tired and hungry that they sat down in a hollow tree and went to sleep.

In the morning when they awoke, the sun had risen high above the trees, and shone warm upon the hollow tree. Then Hansel said, "Sister, I am very thirsty; if I could find a brook, I would go and drink, and fetch you some water too. Listen, I think I hear the sound of one." Then Hansel rose up and took Grettel by the hand and went in search of the brook. But their cruel step-mother was a fairy, and had followed them into the wood to work them mischief: and when they had found a brook that ran sparkling over the pebbles, Hansel wanted to drink; but Grettel thought she heard the brook, as it babbled along, say, "Whoever drinks here will be turned into a tiger." Then she cried out, "Ah, brother! do not drink, or you will be turned into a wild beast and tear me to pieces." Then Hansel yielded, although he was parched with thirst. "I will wait," said he, "for the next brook." But when they came to the next, Grettel listened again, and thought she heard, "Whoever drinks here will become a wolf." Then she cried out, "Brother, brother, do not drink, or you will become a wolf and eat me." So he did not drink, but said, "I will wait for the next brook; there I must drink, say what you will, I am so thirsty."

As they came to the third brook, Grettel listened, and heard, "Whoever drinks here will become a fawn." "Ah, brother!" said she, "do not drink, or you will be turned into a fawn and run away from me." But Hansel had already stooped down upon his knees, and the moment he put his lips into the water he was turned into a fawn.

Grettel wept bitterly over the poor creature, and the tears too rolled down his eyes as he laid himself beside her. Then she said, "Rest in peace, dear fawn, I will never never leave thee." So she took off her golden necklace and put it round his neck, and plucked some rushes and plaited them into a soft string to fasten to it; and led the poor little thing by her side farther into the wood.

After they had travelled a long way, they came at last to a little cottage; and Grettel, having looked in and seen that it was quite empty, thought to herself, "We can stay and live here." Then she went and gathered leaves and moss to make a soft bed for the fawn: and every morning she went out and plucked nuts, roots, and berries for herself, and sweet shrubs and tender grass for her companion; and it ate out of her hand, and was pleased, and played and frisked about her. In the evening, when Grettel was tired, and had said her prayers, she laid her head upon the fawn for her pillow, and slept: and if poor Hansel could but have his right form again, they thought they should lead a very happy life.

They lived thus a long while in the wood by themselves, till it chanced that the king of that country came to hold a great hunt there. And when the fawn heard all around the echoing of the horns, and the baying of the dogs, and the merry shouts of the huntsmen, he wished very much to go and see what was going on. "Ah sister! sister!" said he, "let me go out into the wood, I can stay no longer." And he begged so long, that she at last agreed to let him go. "But," said she, "be sure to come to me in the evening: I shall shut up the door to keep out those wild huntsmen; but if you tap at it, and say, "Sister, let me in," I shall know you; but if you don't speak, I shall keep the door fast." Then away sprang the fawn, and frisked and bounded along in the open air. The king and his huntsmen saw the beautiful creature, and followed but could not overtake him; for when they thought they were sure of their prize, he sprung over the bushes and was out of sight in a moment.

As it grew dark he came running home to the hut, and tapped, and said "Sister, sister, let me in." Then she opened the little door, and in he jumped and slept soundly all night on his soft bed.

Next morning the hunt began again; and when he heard the huntsmen's horns, he said, "Sister, open the door for me, I must go again." Then she let him out, and said, "Come back in the evening, and remember what you are to say." When the king and the huntsmen saw the fawn with the golden collar again, they gave him chase; but he was too quick for them. The chase lasted the whole day; but at last the huntsmen nearly surrounded him, and one of them wounded him in the foot, so that he became sadly lame and could hardly crawl home. The man who had wounded him followed close behind, and hid himself, and heard the little fawn say, "Sister, sister, let me in:" upon which the door opened and soon shut again. The huntsman marked all well, and went to the king and told him what he had seen and heard; then the king said, "To-morrow we will have another chase."

Grettel was very much frightened when she saw that her dear little fawn was wounded; but she washed the blood away and put some healing herbs on it, and said, "Now go to bed, dear fawn, and you will soon be well again." The wound was so small, that in the morning there was nothing to be seen of it; and when the horn blew, the little creature said, "I can't stay here, I must go and look on; I will take care that none of them shall catch me." But Grettel said, "I am sure they will kill you this time, I will not let you go." "I shall die of vexation," answered he, "if you keep me here; when I hear the horns, I feel as if I could fly." Then Grettel was forced to let him go; so she opened the door with a heavy heart, and he bounded out gaily into the wood.

When the king saw him, he said to his huntsman, "Now chase him all day long till you catch him; but let none of you do him any harm." The sun set, however, without their being able to overtake him, and the king called away the huntsmen, and said to the one who had watched, "Now come and show me the little hut." So they went to the door and tapped, and said, "Sister, sister, let me in." Then the door opened and the king went in, and there stood a maiden more lovely than any he had ever seen. Grettel was frightened to see that it was not her fawn, but a king with a golden crown, that was come into her hut: however, he spoke kindly to her, and took her hand, and said, "Will you come with me to my castle and be my wife?" "Yes," said the maiden; "but my fawn must go with me, I cannot part with that." "Well," said the king, "he shall come and live with you all your life, and want for nothing." Just at that moment in sprung the little fawn; and his sister tied the string to his neck, and they left the hut in the wood together.

Then the king took Grettel to his palace, and celebrated the marriage in great state. And she told the king all her story; and he sent for the fairy and punished her: and the fawn was changed into Hansel again, and he and his sister loved one another, and lived happily together all their days.

# THE FROG-PRINCE

One fine evening a young princess went into a wood, and sat down by the side of a cool spring of water. She had a golden ball in her hand, which was her favourite plaything, and she amused herself with tossing it into the air and catching it again as it fell. After a time she threw it up so high that when she stretched out her hand to catch it, the ball bounded away and rolled along upon the ground, till at last it fell into the spring. The princess looked into the spring after her ball; but it was very deep, so deep that she could not see the bottom of it. Then she began to lament her loss, and said, "Alas! if I could only get my ball again, I would give all my fine clothes and jewels, and every thing that I have in the world." Whilst she was speaking a frog put its head out of the water, and said, "Princess, why do you weep so bitterly?" "Alas!" said she, "what can you do for me, you nasty frog? My golden ball has fallen into the spring." The frog said, "I want not your pearls and jewels and fine clothes; but if you will love me and let me live with you, and eat from your little golden plate, and sleep upon your little bed, I will bring you your ball again." "What nonsense," thought the princess," this silly frog is talking! He can never get out of the well: however, he may be able to get my ball for me; and therefore I will promise him what he asks." So she said to the frog, "Well, if you will bring me my ball, I promise to do all you require." Then the frog put his head down, and dived deep under the water; and after a little while he came up again with the ball in his mouth, and threw it on the ground. As soon as the young princess saw her ball, she ran to pick it up, and was so overjoyed to have it in her hand again, that she never thought of the frog, but ran home with it as fast as she could. The frog called after her, "Stay, princess, and take me with you as you promised;" but she did not stop to hear a word.

The next day, just as the princess had sat down to dinner, she heard a strange noise, tap-tap, as if somebody was coming up the marble staircase; and soon afterwards something knocked gently at the door, and said,

"Open the door, my princess dear,
Open the door to thy true love here!
And mind the words that thou and I said
By the fountain cool in the greenwood shade."

Then the princess ran to the door and opened it, and there she saw the frog, whom she had quite forgotten; she was terribly frightened, and shutting the door as fast as she could, came back to her seat. The king her father asked her what had frightened her. "There is a nasty frog," said she, "at the door, who lifted my ball out of the spring this morning: I promised him that he should live with me here, thinking that he could never get out of the spring; but there he is at the door and wants to come in!" While she

35

was speaking the frog knocked again at the door, and said,

> "Open the door, my princess dear,
> Open the door to thy true love here!
> And mind the words that thou and I said
> By the fountain cool in the greenwood shade."

The king said to the young princess, "As you have made a promise, you must keep it; so go and let him in." She did so, and the frog hopped into the room, and came up close to the table. "Pray lift me upon a chair," said he to the princess, "and let me sit next to you." As soon as she had done this, the frog said, "Put your plate closer to me that I may eat out of it." This she did, and when he had eaten as much as he could, he said, "Now I am tired; carry me up stairs and put me into your little bed." And the princess took him up in her hand and put him upon the pillow of her own little bed, where he slept all night long. As soon as it was light he jumped up, hopped down stairs, and went out of the house. "Now," thought the princess, "he is gone, and I shall be troubled with him no more."

But she was mistaken; for when night came again, she heard the same tapping at the door, and when she opened it, the frog came in and slept upon her pillow as before till the morning broke: and the third night he did the same; but when the princess awoke on the following morning, she was astonished to see, instead of the frog, a handsome prince gazing on her with the most beautiful eyes that ever were seen, and standing at the head of her bed.

He told her that he had been enchanted by a malicious fairy, who had changed him into the form of a frog, in which he was fated to remain till some princess should take him out of the spring and let him sleep upon her bed for three nights. "You," said the prince, "have broken this cruel charm, and now I have nothing to wish for but that you should go with me into my father's kingdom, where I will marry you, and love you as long as you live."

The young princess, you may be sure, was not long in giving her consent; and as they spoke a splendid carriage drove up with eight beautiful horses decked with plumes of feathers and golden harness, and behind rode the prince's servant, the faithful Henry, who had bewailed the misfortune of his dear master so long and bitterly that his heart had well nigh burst. Then all set out full of joy for the Prince's kingdom; where they arrived safely, and lived happily a great many years.

# RUMPEL-STILTS-KIN

In a certain kingdom once lived a poor miller who had a very beautiful daughter. She was moreover exceedingly shrewd and clever; and the miller was so vain and proud of her, that he one day told the king of the land that his daughter could spin gold out of straw. Now this king was very fond of money; and when he heard the miller's boast, his avarice was excited, and he ordered the girl to be brought before him. Then he led her to a chamber where there was a great quantity of straw, gave her a spinning-wheel, and said, "All this must be spun into gold before morning, as you value your life." It was in vain that the poor maiden declared that she could do no such thing, the chamber was locked and she remained alone.

She sat down in one corner of the room and began to lament over her hard fate, when on a sudden the door opened, and a droll-looking little man hobbled in, and said, "Good morrow to you, my good lass, what are you weeping for?" "Alas!" answered she, "I must spin this straw into gold, and I know not how." "What will you give me," said the little man, "to do it for you?" "My necklace," replied the maiden. He took her at her word, and sat himself down to the wheel; round about it went merrily, and presently the work was done and the gold all spun.

When the king came and saw this, he was greatly astonished and pleased; but his heart grew still more greedy of gain, and he shut up the poor miller's daughter again with a fresh task. Then she knew not what to do, and sat down once more to weep; but the little man presently opened the door, and said, "What will you give me to do your task?" "The ring on my finger," replied she. So her little friend took the ring, and began to work at the wheel, till by the morning all was finished again.

The king was vastly delighted to see all this glittering treasure; but still he was not satisfied, and took the miller's daughter into a yet larger room, and said, "All this must be spun to-night; and if you succeed, you shall be my queen." As soon as she was alone the dwarf came in, and said, "What will you give me to spin gold for you this third time?" "I have nothing left," said she. "Then promise me," said the little man, "your first little child when you are queen." "That may never be," thought the miller's daughter; and as she knew no other way to get her task done, she promised him what he asked, and he spun once more the whole heap of gold. The king came in the morning, and finding all he wanted, married her, and so the miller's daughter really became queen.

At the birth of her first little child the queen rejoiced very much, and forgot the little man and her promise; but one day he came into her chamber and reminded her of it. Then she grieved sorely at her misfortune, and offered him all the treasures of the kingdom in exchange; but in vain, till at last her tears softened him, and he said, "I will give you three days' grace, and if during that time you tell me my name, you shall keep your child."

Now the queen lay awake all night, thinking of all the odd names that she had ever heard, and dispatched messengers all over the land to inquire after new ones. The next day the little man came, and she began with Timothy, Benjamin, Jeremiah, and all the names she could remember; but to all of them he said, "That's not my name."

The second day she began with all the comical names she could hear of, Bandy-legs, Hunch-back, Crookshanks, and so on, but the little gentleman still said to every one of them, "That's not my name."

The third day came back one of the messengers, and said, "I can hear of no one other name; but yesterday, as I was climbing a high hill among the trees of the forest where the fox and the hare bid each other good night, I saw a little hut, and before the hut burnt a fire, and round about the fire danced a funny little man upon one leg, and sung

> "Merrily the feast I'll make,
> Today I'll brew, to-morrow bake;
> Merrily I'll dance and sing,
> For next day will a stranger bring:
> Little does my lady dream
> Rumpel-Stilts-Kin is my name!"

When the queen heard this, she jumped for joy, and as soon as her little visitor came, and said, "Now, lady, what is my name?" "Is it John?" asked she. "No!" "Is it Tom?" "No!"

> "Can your name be Rumpel-Stilts-Kin?"

"Some witch told you that! Some witch told you that!" cried the little man, and dashed his right foot in a rage so deep into the floor, that he was forced to lay hold of it with both hands to pull it out. Then he made the best of his way off, while every body laughed at him for having had all his trouble for nothing.

# THE FISHERMAN AND HIS WIFE

There was once a fisherman who lived with his wife in a ditch, close by the sea-side. The fisherman used to go out all day a-fishing; and one day, as he sat on the shore with his rod, looking at the shining water and watching his line, all on a sudden his float was dragged away deep under the sea: and in drawing it up he pulled a great fish out of the water. The fish said to him, "Pray let me live: I am not a real fish; I am an enchanted prince, put me in the water again, and let me go." "Oh!" said the man, "you need not make so many words about the matter; I wish to have nothing to do with a fish that can talk; so swim away as soon as you please." Then he put him back into the water, and the fish darted straight down to the bottom, and left a long streak of blood behind him.

When the fisherman went home to his wife in the ditch, he told her how he had caught a great fish, and how it had told him it was an enchanted prince, and that on hearing it speak he had let it go again. "Did you not ask it for any thing?" said the wife. "No," said the man, "what should I ask for?" "Ah!" said the wife, "we live very wretchedly here in this nasty stinking ditch; do go back, and tell the fish we want a little cottage."

The fisherman did not much like the business: however, he went to the sea, and when he came there the water looked all yellow and green. And he stood at the water's edge, and said,

41

"O man of the sea!
Come listen to me,
For Alice my wife,
The plague of my life,
Has sent me to beg a boon of thee!"

Then the fish came swimming to him, and said, "Well, what does she want?" "Ah!" answered the fisherman, "my wife says that when I had caught you, I ought to have asked you for something before I let you go again; she does not like living any longer in the ditch, and wants a little cottage." "Go home, then," said the fish, "she is in the cottage already." So the man went home, and saw his wife standing at the door of a cottage. "Come in, come in," said she; "is not this much better than the ditch?" And there was a parlour, and a bed-chamber, and a kitchen; and behind the cottage there was a little garden with all sorts of flowers and fruits, and a court-yard full of ducks and chickens. "Ah!" said the fisherman, "how happily we shall live!" "We will try to do so at least," said his wife.

Every thing went right for a week or two, and then Dame Alice said, "Husband, there is not room enough in this cottage, the court-yard and garden are a great deal too small; I should like to have a large stone castle to live in; so go to the fish again, and tell him to give us a castle." "Wife," said the fisherman, "I don't like to go to him again, for perhaps he will be angry; we ought to be content with the cottage." "Nonsense!" said the wife; "he will do it very willingly; go along, and try."

The fisherman went; but his heart was very heavy: and when he came to the sea, it looked blue and

gloomy, though it was quite calm, and he went close
to it, and said,

"O man of the sea!
Come listen to me,
For Alice my wife,
The plague of my life,
Hath sent me to beg a boon of thee!"

"Well, what does she want now?" said the fish. "Ah!"
said the man very sorrowfully, "my wife wants to live
in a stone castle." "Go home then," said the fish, "she
is standing at the door of it already." So away went the
fisherman, and found his wife standing before a great
castle. "See," said she, "is not this grand?" With that
they went into the castle together, and found a great
many servants there, and the rooms all richly furnished
and full of golden chairs and tables; and behind the
castle was a garden, and a wood half a mile long, full
of sheep, and goats, and hares, and deer; and in the
court-yard were stables and cow-houses. "Well," said
the man, "now will we live contented and happy in
this beautiful castle for the rest of our lives." "Perhaps
we may," said the wife; "but let us consider and sleep
upon it before we make up our minds:" so they went
to bed.

The next morning, when Dame Alice awoke, it was
broad day-light, and she jogged the fisherman with her
elbow, and said, "Get up, husband, and bestir yourself,
for we must be king of all the land." "Wife, wife," said
the man, "why should we wish to be king? I will not be
king." "Then I will," said Alice. "But, wife," answered
the fisherman, "how can you be king? the fish cannot

make you a king." "Husband," said she, "say no more about it, but go and try; I will be king!" So the man went away, quite sorrowful to think that his wife should want to be king. The sea looked a dark grey colour, and was covered with foam as he cried out,

> "O man of the sea!
> Come listen to me,
> For Alice my wife,
> The plague of my life,
> Hath sent me to beg a boon of thee!"

"Well, what would she have now?" said the fish. "Alas!" said the man, "my wife wants to be king." "Go home," said the fish; "she is king already."

Then the fisherman went home; and as he came close to the palace, he saw a troop of soldiers, and heard the sound of drums and trumpets; and when he entered in, he saw his wife sitting on a high throne of gold and diamonds, with a golden crown upon her head; and on each side of her stood six beautiful maidens, each a head taller than the other. "Well, wife," said the fisherman, "are you king?" "Yes," said she, "I am king." And when he had looked at her for a long time, he said, "Ah, wife! what a fine thing it is to be king! now we shall never have any thing more to wish for." "I don't know how that may be," said she; "never is a long time. I am king, 'tis true, but I begin to be tired of it, and I think I should like to be emperor." "Alas, wife! why should you wish to be emperor?" said the fisherman. "Husband," said she, "go to the fish; I say I will be emperor." "Ah, wife!" replied the fisherman, "the fish cannot make an emperor, and I should not like to ask for such a thing." "I am king," said Alice, "and you are my slave, so go directly!" So the fisherman was obliged to go; and he muttered as he went along. "This will come to no good, it is too much to ask, the fish will be tired at last, and then we shall repent of what we have done." He soon arrived at the sea, and the water was quite black and muddy, and a mighty whirlwind blew over it; but he went to the shore, and said,

> "O man of the sea!
> Come listen to me,
> For Alice my wife,
> The plague of my life,
> Hath sent me to beg a boon of thee!"

"What would she have now!" said the fish. "Ah!" said the fisherman, "she wants to be emperor." "Go home," said the fish; "she is emperor already."

So he went home again; and as he came near he saw his wife sitting on a very lofty throne made of solid gold, with a great crown on her head full two yards high, and on each side of her stood her guards and attendants in a row, each one smaller than the other, from the tallest giant down to a little dwarf no bigger than my finger. And before her stood princes, and dukes, and earls: and the fisherman went up to her and said, "Wife, are you emperor?" "Yes," said she, "I am emperor." "Ah!" said the man as he gazed upon her, "what a fine thing it is to be emperor!" "Husband," said she, "why should we stay at being emperor; I will be pope next." "O wife, wife!" said he, "how can you be pope? there is but one pope at a time in Christendom." "Husband," said she, "I will be pope this very day." "But," replied the husband, "the fish cannot make you pope." "What nonsense!" said she, "if he can make an emperor, he can make a pope, go and try him." So the fisherman went. But when he came to the shore the wind was raging, and the sea was tossed up and down like boiling water, and the ships were in the greatest distress and danced upon the waves most fearfully; in the middle of the sky there was a little blue, but towards the south it was all red as if a dreadful storm was rising. At this the fisherman was terribly frightened, and trembled, so that his knees knocked together: but he went to the shore and said,

"O man of the sea!
Come listen to me,
For Alice my wife,
The plague of my life,
Hath sent me to beg a boon of thee!"

"What does she want now?" said the fish. "Ah!" said the fisherman, "my wife wants to be pope." "Go home," said the fish, "she is pope already."

Then the fisherman went home, and found his wife sitting on a throne that was two miles high; and she had three great crowns on her head, and around stood all the pomp and power of the Church; and on each side were two rows of burning lights, of all sizes, the greatest as large as the highest and biggest tower in the world, and the least no larger than a small rushlight. "Wife," said the fisherman as he looked at all this grandeur, "Are you pope?" "Yes," said she, "I am pope." "Well, wife," replied he, "it is a grand thing to be pope; and now you must be content, for you can be nothing greater." "I will consider of that," said the wife. Then they went to bed:

but Dame Alice could not sleep all night for thinking what she should be next. At last morning came, and the sun rose. "Ha!" thought she as she looked at it through the window, "cannot I prevent the sun rising?" At this she was very angry, and she wakened her husband, and said, "Husband, go to the fish and tell him I want to be lord of the sun and moon." The fisherman was half asleep, but the thought frightened him so much, that he started and fell out of bed. "Alas, wife!" said he, "cannot you be content to be pope?" "No," said she, "I am very uneasy, and cannot bear to see the sun and moon rise without my leave. Go to the fish directly."

Then the man went trembling for fear; and as he was going down to the shore a dreadful storm arose, so that the trees and the rocks shook; and the heavens became black, and the lightning played, and the thunder rolled; and you might have seen in the sea great black waves like mountains with a white crown of foam upon them; and the fisherman said,

> "O man of the sea!
> Come listen to me,
> For Alice my wife,
> The plague of my life,
> Hath sent me to beg a boon of thee!"

"What does she want now?" said the fish. "Ah!" said he, "she wants to be lord of the sun and moon." "Go home," said the fish, "to your ditch again!" and there they live to this very day.

47

# THE GOLDEN BIRD

A certain king had a beautiful garden, and in the garden stood a tree which bore golden apples. These apples were always counted, and about the time when they began to grow ripe it was found that every night one of them was gone. The king became very angry at this, and ordered the gardener to keep watch all night under the tree. The gardener set his eldest son to watch; but about twelve o'clock he fell asleep, and in the morning another of the apples was missing. Then the second son was ordered to watch; and at midnight he too fell asleep, and in the morning another apple was gone. Then the third son offered to keep watch; but the gardener at first would not let him, for fear some harm should come to him: however, at last he consented, and the young man laid himself under the tree to watch. As the clock struck twelve he heard a rustling noise in the air, and a bird came flying that was of pure gold; and as it was snapping at one of the apples with its beak, the gardener's son jumped up and shot an arrow at it. But the arrow did the bird no harm; only it dropped a golden feather from its tail, and then flew away. The golden feather was brought to the king in the morning, and all the council was called together. Every one agreed that it was worth more than all the wealth of the kingdom: but the king said, "One feather is of no use to me, I must have the whole bird."

Then the gardener's eldest son set out and thought to find the golden bird very easily; and when he had gone but a little way, he came to a wood, and by the side of the wood he saw a fox sitting; so he took his bow and made ready to shoot at it. Then the fox said, "Do not shoot me, for I will give you good counsel; I know what your business is, and that you want to find the golden bird. You will reach a village in the evening; and when you get there, you will see two inns opposite to each other, one of which is very pleasant and beautiful to look at: go not in there, but rest for the night in the other, though it may appear to you to be very poor and mean." But the son thought to himself, "What can such a beast as this know about the matter?" So he shot his arrow at the fox; but he missed it, and it set up its tail above its back and ran into the wood. Then he went his way, and in the evening came to the village where the two inns were; and in one of these were people singing, and dancing, and feasting; but the other looked very dirty, and poor. "I should be very silly," said he, "if I went to that shabby house, and left this charming place;" so he went into the smart house, and ate and drank at his ease, and forgot the bird, and his country too.

Time passed on; and as the eldest son did not come back, and no tidings were heard of him, the second son set out, and the same thing happened to him. He met the fox, who gave him the same good advice: but when he came to the two inns, his eldest brother was standing at the window where the merrymaking was, and called to him to come in; and he could not withstand the temptation, but went in, and forgot the golden bird and his country in the same manner.

Time passed on again, and the youngest son too wished to set out into the wide world to seek for the golden bird; but his father would not listen to it for a

49

long while, for he was very fond of his son, and was afraid that some ill luck might happen to him also, and prevent his coming back. However, at last it was agreed he should go, for he would not rest at home; and as he came to the wood, he met the fox, and heard the same good counsel. But he was thankful to the fox, and did not attempt his life as his brothers had done; so the fox said, "Sit upon my tail, and you will travel faster." So he sat down, and the fox began to run, and away they went over stock and stone so quick that their hair whistled in the wind.

When they came to the village, the son followed the fox's counsel, and without looking about him went to the shabby inn and rested there all night at his ease. In the morning came the fox again and met him as he was beginning his journey, and said, "Go straight forward, till you come to a castle, before which lie a whole troop of soldiers fast asleep and snoring: take no notice of them, but go into the castle and pass on and on till you come to a room, where the golden bird sits in a wooden cage; close by it stands a beautiful golden cage; but do not try to take the bird out of the shabby cage and put it into the handsome one, otherwise you will repent it." Then the fox stretched out his tail again, and the young man sat himself down, and away they went over stock and stone till their hair whistled in the wind.

Before the castle gate all was as the fox had said: so the son went in and found the chamber where the golden bird hung in a wooden cage, and below stood the golden cage, and the three golden apples that had been lost were lying close by it. Then thought he to himself, "It will be a very droll thing to bring away such a fine bird in this shabby cage;" so he opened the door and took hold of it and put it into the golden cage. But the bird set up such a loud scream that all the soldiers awoke, and they took him prisoner and carried him before the king. The next morning the court sat to judge him; and when all was heard, it sentenced him to die, unless he should bring the king the golden horse which could run as swiftly as the wind; and if he did this, he was to have the golden bird given him for his own.

So he set out once more on his journey, sighing, and in great despair, when on a sudden his good friend the fox met him, and said, "You see now what has happened on account of your not listening to my counsel. I will still, however, tell you how to find the golden horse, if you will do as I bid you. You must go straight on till you come to the castle where the horse stands in his stall: by his side will lie the groom fast asleep and snoring: take away the horse quietly, but be sure to put the old leathern saddle upon him, and not the golden one that is close by it." Then the son sat down on the fox's tail, and away they went over stock and stone till their hair whistled in the wind.

All went right, and the groom lay snoring with his hand upon the golden saddle. But when the son looked at the horse, he thought it a great pity to put the leathern saddle upon it. "I will give him the good one," said he; "I am sure he deserves it." As he took up the golden saddle the groom awoke and cried out so loud, that all the guards ran in and took him prisoner, and in the morning he was again brought before the court to be judged, and was sentenced to die. But it was agreed, that, if he could bring thither the beautiful princess, he should live, and have the bird and the horse given him for his own.

Then he went his way again very sorrowful; but the old fox came and said, "Why did not you listen to me? If you had, you would have carried away both the bird and the horse; yet will I once more give you counsel. Go straight on, and in the evening you will arrive at a castle. At twelve o'clock at night the princess goes to the bathing-house: go up to her and give her a kiss, and she will let you lead her away; but take care you do not suffer her to go and take leave of her father and mother." Then the fox stretched out his tail, and so away they went over stock and stone till their hair whistled again.

As they came to the castle, all was as the fox had said, and at twelve o'clock the young man met the princess going to the bath and gave her the kiss, and she agreed to run away with him, but begged with many tears that he would let her take leave of her father. At first he refused, but she wept still more and more, and fell at his feet, till at last he consented; but the moment she came to her father's house the guards awoke and he was taken prisoner again.

Then he was brought before the king, and the king said, "You shall never have my daughter unless in eight days you dig away the hill that stops the view from my window." Now this hill was so big that the whole world could not take it away: and when he had worked for seven days, and had done very little, the fox came and said, "Lie down and go to sleep; I will work for you." And in the morning he awoke and the hill was gone; so he went merrily to the king, and told him that now that it was removed he must give him the princess.

Then the king was obliged to keep his word, and away went the young man and the princess; and the fox came and said to him, "We will have all three, the princess, the horse, and the bird." "Ah!" said the young man, "that would be a great thing, but how can you contrive it?"

"If you will only listen," said the fox, "it can soon be done. When you come to the king, and he asks for the beautiful princess, you must say, "Here she is!" Then he will be very joyful; and you will mount the golden horse that they are to give you, and put out your hand to take leave of them; but shake hands with the princess last. Then lift her quickly on to the horse behind you; clap your spurs to his side, and gallop away as fast as you can."

All went right: then the fox said, "When you come to the castle where the bird is, I will stay with the princess at the door, and you will ride in and speak to the king; and when he sees that it is the right horse, he will bring out the bird; but you must sit still, and say that you want to look at it, to see whether it is the true golden bird; and when you get it into your hand, ride away."

This, too, happened as the fox said; they carried off the bird, the princess mounted again, and they rode on to a great wood. Then the fox came, and said, "Pray kill me, and cut off my head and my feet." But the young man refused to do it: so the fox said, "I will at any rate give you good counsel: beware of two things; ransom no one from the gallows, and sit down by the side of no river." Then away he went. "Well," thought the young man, "it is no hard matter to keep that advice."

He rode on with the princess, till at last he came to the village where he had left his two brothers. And there he heard a great noise and uproar; and when he asked what was the matter, the people said, "Two men are going to be hanged." As he came nearer, he saw that the two

53

men were his brothers, who had turned robbers; so he said, "Cannot they in any way be saved?" But the people said "No," unless he would bestow all his money upon the rascals and buy their liberty. Then he did not stay to think about the matter, but paid what was asked, and his brothers were given up, and went on with him towards their home.

And as they came to the wood where the fox first met them, it was so cool and pleasant that the two brothers said, "Let us sit down by the side of the river, and rest a while, to eat and drink." So he said, "Yes," and forgot the fox's counsel, and sat down on the side of the river; and while he suspected nothing, they came behind, and threw him down the bank, and took the princess, the horse, and the bird, and went home to the king their master, and said, "All this have we won by our labour." Then there was great rejoicing made; but the horse would not eat, the bird would not sing, and the princess wept.

The youngest son fell to the bottom of the river's bed: luckily it was nearly dry, but his bones were almost broken, and the bank was so steep that he could find no way to get out. Then the old fox came once more, and scolded him for not following his advice; otherwise no evil would have befallen him: "Yet," said he, "I cannot leave you here, so lay hold of my tail and hold fast." Then he pulled him out of the river, and said to him, as he got upon the bank, "Your brothers have set watch to kill you, if they find you in the kingdom." So he dressed himself as a poor man, and came secretly to the king's court, and was scarcely within the doors when the horse began to eat, and the bird to sing, and the princess left off weeping. Then he went to the king, and told him all his brothers' roguery; and they were seized and punished, and he had the princess given to him again; and after the king's death he was heir to his kingdom.

A long while after, he went to walk one day in the wood, and the old fox met him, and besought him with tears in his eyes to kill him, and cut off his head and feet. And at last he did so, and in a moment the fox was changed into a man, and turned out to be the brother of the princess, who had been lost a great many many years.

# THE TRAVELLING MUSICIANS

An honest farmer had once an ass, that had been a faithful servant to him a great many years, but was now growing old and every day more and more unfit for work. His master therefore was tired of keeping him and began to think of putting an end to him; but the ass, who saw that some mischief was in the wind, took himself slyly off, and began his journey towards the great city, "for there," thought he, "I may turn musician."

After he had travelled a little way, he spied a dog lying by the road-side and panting as if he were very tired. "What makes you pant so, my friend?" said the ass. "Alas!" said the dog, "my master was going to knock me on the head, because I am old and weak, and can no longer make myself useful to him in hunting; so I ran away: but what can I do to earn my livelihood?" "Hark ye!" said the ass, "I am going to the great city to turn musician: suppose you go with me, and try what you can do in the same way?" The dog said he was willing, and they jogged on together.

They had not gone far before they saw a cat sitting in the middle of the road and making a most rueful face. "Pray, my good lady," said the ass, "what's the matter with you? you look quite out of spirits!" "Ah me!" said the cat, "how can one be in good spirits when one's life is in danger? Because I am beginning to grow old, and had rather lie at my ease by the fire than run about the house after the mice, my mistress laid hold of me, and was going to drown me; and though I have been lucky enough to get away from her, I do not know what I am to live upon." "O!" said the ass, "by all means go with us to the great city; you are a good night singer, and may make your fortune as a musician." The cat was pleased with the thought, and joined the party.

Soon afterwards, as they were passing by a farmyard, they saw a cock perched upon a gate, and screaming out with all his might and main. "Bravo!" said the ass; "upon my word you make a famous noise; pray what is all this about?" "Why," said the cock, "I was just now saying that we should have fine weather for our washing-day, and yet my mistress and the cook don't thank me for my pains, but threaten to cut off my head tomorrow, and make broth of me for the guests that are coming on Sunday" "Heaven forbid" said the ass; "come with us, Master Chanticleer; it will be better, at any rate, than staying here to have your head cut off! Besides, who knows? If we take care to sing in tune, we may get up some kind of a concert: so come along with us." "With all my heart," said the cock: so they all four went on jollily together.

They could not, however, reach the great city the first day; so when night came on, they went into a wood to sleep. The ass and the dog laid themselves down under a great tree, and the cat climbed up into the branches; while the cock, thinking that the higher he sat the safer he should be, flew up the very top of the tree, and then, according to his custom, before he went to sleep, looked out on all sides of him to see that every thing was well. In doing this, he saw afar off something bright and shining; and calling to his companions said, "There must be a house no great way off, for I see a light." "If that be the case," said the ass, "we had better change our quarters, for our lodging is not the best in the world!" "Besides," added the dog, "I should not be the worse for a bone or two, or a bit of meat." So they walked off together towards the spot where Chanticleer had seen the light; and as they drew near, it became larger and brighter, till they at last came close to a house in which a gang of robbers lived.

The ass, being the tallest of the company, marched up to the window and peeped in. "Well, Donkey," said Chanticleer, "what do you see?" "What do I see?" replied the ass, "why I see a table spread with all kinds of good things, and robbers sitting round it making merry." "That would be a noble lodging for us," said the cock. "Yes," said the ass, "if we could only get in:" so they consulted together how they should contrive to get the robbers out; and at last they hit upon a plan. The ass placed himself upright on his hind-legs, with his fore-feet resting against the window; the dog got upon his back; the cat scrambled up to the dog's shoulders, and the cock flew up and sat upon the cat's head. When all was ready, a signal was given, and they began their music. The ass brayed, the dog barked, the cat mewed, and the cock screamed; and then they all broke through the window at once, and came tumbling into the room, amongst the broken glass, with a most hideous clatter! The robbers, who had been not a little frightened by the opening concert, had now no doubt that some frightful hobgoblin had broken in upon them, and scampered away as fast as they could.

The coast once clear, our travellers soon sat down, and dispatched what the robbers had left, with as much eagerness as if they had not expected to eat again for a month. As soon as they had satisfied themselves, they put out the lights, and each once more sought out a resting-place to his own liking. The donkey laid himself down upon a heap of straw in the yard; the dog stretched himself upon a mat behind the door; the cat rolled herself up on the hearth before the warm ashes; and the cock perched upon a beam on top of the house; and, as they were all rather tired with their journey, they soon fell asleep.

But about midnight, when the robbers saw from afar that the lights were out and that all seemed quiet, they began to think that they had been in too great a hurry to run away; and one of them, who was bolder than the rest, went to see what was going on. Finding every thing still, he marched into the kitchen, and groped about till he found a match in order to light a candle; and then, espying the glittering fiery eyes of the cat, he mistook them for live coals, and held the match to them to light it. But the cat, not understanding this joke, sprung at his face, and spit, and scratched at him. This frightened him dreadfully, and away he ran to the back door; but there the dog jumped up and bit him in the leg; and as he was crossing over the yard the ass kicked him; and the cock, who had been awakened by the noise, crowed with all his might. At this the robber ran back as fast as he could to his comrades, and told the captain "how a horrid witch had got into the house, and had spit at him and scratched his face with her long bony fingers; how a man with a knife in his hand had hidden himself behind the door, and stabbed him in the leg; how a black monster stood in the yard and struck him with a club, and how the devil sat upon the top of the house and cried out, "Throw the rascal up here!" After this the robbers never dared to go back to the house: but the musicians were so pleased with their quarters, that they took up their abode there; and there they are, I dare say, at this very day.


# HANS IN LUCK


Hans had served his master seven years, and at last said to him, "Master, my time is up, I should like to go home and see my mother; so give me my wages." And the master said, "You have been a faithful and good servant, so your pay shall be handsome." Then he gave him a piece of silver that was as big as his head.

Hans took out his pocket-handkerchief, put the piece of silver into it, threw it over his shoulder, and jogged off homewards. As he went lazily on, dragging one foot after another, a man came in sight, trotting along gaily on a capital horse. "Ah!" said Hans aloud, "what a fine thing it is to ride on horseback! there he sits as if he was at home in his chair; he trips against no stones, spares his shoes, and yet gets on he hardly knows how." The horseman heard this, and said, "Well, Hans, why do you go on foot then?" "Ah!" said he, "I have this load to carry; to be sure it is silver, but it is so heavy that I can't hold up my head, and it hurts my shoulder sadly." "What do you say to changing?" said the horseman; "I will give you my horse, and you shall give me the silver." "With all my heart," said Hans: "but I tell you one thing,—you'll have a weary task to drag it along." The horseman got off, took the silver, helped Hans up, gave him the bridle into his hand, and said, "When you want to go very fast, you must smack your lips loud, and cry 'Jip'."

Hans was delighted as he sat on the horse, and rode merrily on. After a time he thought he should like to go a little faster, so he smacked his lips, and cried "Jip". Away went the horse full gallop; and before Hans knew what he was about, he was thrown off, and lay in a ditch by the roadside; and his horse would have run off, if a shepherd who was coming by, driving a cow, had not stopt it. Hans soon came to himself, and got upon his legs again. He was sadly vexed, and said to the shepherd, "This riding is no joke when a man gets on a beast like this, that stumbles and flings him off as if he would break his neck. However, I'm off now once for all: I like your cow a great deal better; one can walk along at one's leisure behind her, and have milk, butter, and cheese, every day into the bargain. What would I give to have such a cow!" "Well," said the shepherd, "if you are so fond of her, I will change my cow for your horse." "Done!" said Hans merrily. The shepherd jumped upon the horse, and away he rode.

Hans drove off his cow quietly, and thought his

bargain a very lucky one. "If I have only a piece of bread (and I certainly shall be able to get that), I can, whenever I like, eat my butter and cheese with it; and when I am thirsty I can milk my cow and drink the milk: what can I wish for more?" When he came to an inn, he halted, ate up all his bread, and gave away his last penny for a glass of beer: then he drove his cow towards his mother's village; and the heat grew greater as noon came on, till at last he found himself on a wide heath that would take him more than an hour to cross, and he began to be so hot and parched that his tongue clave to the roof of his mouth. "I can find a cure for this," thought he, "now will I milk my cow and quench my thirst;" so he tied her to the stump of a tree, and held his leathern cap to milk into; but not a drop was to be had.

While he was trying his luck and managing the matter very clumsily, the uneasy beast gave him a kick on the head that knocked him down, and there he lay a long while senseless. Luckily a butcher soon came by driving a pig in a wheel-barrow. "What is the matter with you?" said the butcher as he helped him up. Hans told him what had happened, and the butcher gave him a flask, saying. "There, drink and refresh yourself; your cow will give you no milk, she is an old beast good for nothing but the slaughterhouse." "Alas, alas! said Hans, "who would have thought it? If I kill her, what will she be good for? I hate cow-beef, it is not tender enough for me. If it were a pig now, one could do something with it, it would at any rate make some sausages." "Well," said the butcher, "to please you, I'll change, and give you the pig for the cow." "Heaven reward you for your kindness!" said Hans as he gave the butcher the cow, and took the pig off the wheel-barrow, and drove it off, holding it by the string that was tied to its leg.

So on he jogged, and all seemed now to go right with him; he had met with some misfortunes, to be sure; but he was now well repaid for all. The next person he met was a countryman carrying a fine white goose under his arm. The countryman stopped to ask what was o'clock; and Hans told him all his luck, and how he had made so many good bargains. The countryman said he was going to take the goose to a christening; "Feel," said he, "how heavy it is, and yet it is only eight weeks old. Whoever roasts and eats it may cut plenty of fat off it, it has lived so well!" "You're right," said Hans as he weighed it in his hand; "but my pig is no trifle." Meantime the countryman began to look grave, and shook his head. "Hark ye," said he, "my good friend; your pig may get you into a scrape; in the village I just come from, the squire has had a pig stolen out of his stye. I was dreadfully afraid, when I saw you, that you had got the squire's pig; it will be a bad job if they catch you; the least they'll do, will be to throw you into the horsepond."

Poor Hans was sadly frightened. "Good man," cried he, "pray get me out of this scrape; you know this country better than I, take my pig and give me the goose." "I ought to have something into the bargain," said the countryman; "however, I will not bear hard upon you, as you are in trouble." Then he took the string in his hand, and drove off the pig by a side path; while Hans went on the way homewards free from care. "After all," thought he, "I have the best of the bargain: first there will be a capital roast; then the fat will find me in goose grease for six months; and then there are all the beautiful white feathers; I will put them into my pillow, and then I am sure I shall sleep soundly without rocking. How happy my mother will be!"

As he came to the last village, he saw a scissor-grinder, with his wheel, working away, and singing

O'er hill and o'er dale so happy I roam,
Work light and live well, all the world is my home;
Who so blythe, so merry as I?

Hans stood looking for a while, and at last said, "You must be well off, master grinder, you seem so happy at your work." "Yes," said the other, "mine is a golden trade; a good grinder never puts his hand in his pocket without finding money in it:—but where did you get that beautiful goose?" "I did not buy it, but changed a pig for it." "And where did you get the pig?" "I gave a cow for it." "And the cow?" "I gave a horse for it." "And the horse?" "I gave a piece of silver as big as my head for that." "And the silver?" "Oh! I worked hard for that seven long years." "You have thriven well in the world hitherto," said the grinder; "now if you could find money in your pocket whenever you put your hand into it, your fortune would be made." "Very true: but how is that to be managed?" "You must turn grinder like me," said the other; "you only want a grindstone; the rest will come of itself. Here is one that is a little the worse for wear: I would not ask more than the value of your goose for it;—will you buy?" "How can you ask such a question?" replied Hans; "I should be the happiest man in the world, if I could have money whenever I put my hand in my pocket; what could I want more? there's the goose!" "Now," said the grinder, as he gave him a common rough stone that lay by his side, "this is a most capital stone; do but manage it cleverly, and you can make an old nail cut with it."

Hans took the stone and went off with a light heart: his eyes sparkled for joy, and he said to himself, "I must have been born in a lucky hour; every thing that I want or wish for comes to me of itself."

Meantime he began to be tired, for he had been travelling ever since day-break; he was hungry too, for he had given away his last penny in his joy at getting the cow. At last he could go no farther, and the stone tired him terribly; he dragged himself to the side of a pond, that he might drink some water, and rest a while; so he laid the stone carefully by his side on the bank: but as he stooped down to drink, he forgot it, pushed it a little, and down it went plump into the pond. For a while he watched it sinking in the deep clear water, then sprang up for joy, and again fell upon his knees, and thanked heaven with tears in his eyes for its kindness in taking away his only plague, the ugly heavy stone. "How happy am I!" cried he: "no mortal was ever so lucky as I am." Then up he got with a light and merry heart and walked on free from all his troubles, till he reached his mother's house.

# THE TOM-TIT AND THE BEAR

One summer day, as the wolf and the bear were walking together in a wood, they heard a bird singing most delightfully. "Brother," said the bear, "what can that bird be that is singing so sweetly?" "O!" said the wolf, "that is his majesty the king of the birds, we must take care to show him all possible respect." (Now I should tell you that this bird was after all no other than the tom-tit.) "If that is the case," said the bear, "I should like to see the royal palace; so pray come along and show it to me." "Gently, my friend," said the wolf, "we cannot see it just yet, we must wait till the queen comes home."

Soon afterwards the queen came with food in her beak, and she and the king began to feed their young ones. "Now for it!" said the bear; and was about to follow them, to see what was to be seen. "Stop a little, master Bruin," said the wolf, "we must wait now till their majesties are gone again." So they marked the hole where they had seen the nest, and went away. But the bear, being very eager to see the royal palace, soon came back again, and peeping into the nest, saw five or six young birds lying at the bottom of it. "What nonsense!" said Bruin, "this is not a royal palace: I never saw such a filthy place in my life; and you are no royal children, you little base-born brats!" As soon as the young tom-tits heard this they were very angry, and screamed out, "We are not base-born, you stupid bear! our father and mother are honest good sort of people: and depend upon it you shall suffer for your insolence!" At this the wolf and the bear grew frightened, and ran away to their dens. But the young tom-tits kept crying and screaming; and when their father and mother came home and offered them food, they all said, "We will not touch a bit; no, not the leg of a fly, though we should die of hunger, till that rascal Bruin has been punished for calling us base-born brats." "Make yourselves easy, my darlings," said the old king, "you may be sure he shall meet with his deserts."

So he went out and stood before the bear's den, and cried out with a loud voice, "Bruin the bear! thou hast shamefully insulted our lawful children: we therefore hereby declare bloody and cruel war against thee and thine, which shall never cease until thou hast been punished as thou so richly deservest." Now when the bear heard this, he called together the ox, the ass, the stag, and all the beasts of the earth, in order to consult about the means of his defence. And the tom-tit also enlisted on his side all the birds of the air, both great and small, and a very large army of hornets, gnats, bees, and flies, and other insects.

As the time approached when the war was to begin, the tom-tit sent out spies to see who was the commander-in-chief of the enemy's forces; and the gnat, who was by far the cleverest spy of them all, flew backwards and forwards in the wood where the enemy's troops were, and at last hid himself under a leaf on a tree, close by which the orders of the day were given out. And the bear, who was standing so near the tree that the gnat could hear all he said, called to the fox and said, "Reynard, you are the cleverest of all the beasts; therefore you shall be our general and lead us to battle: but we must first agree upon some signal, by which we may know what you want us to do." "Behold," said the fox, "I have a fine, long, bushy tail, which is very like a plume of red feathers, and gives me a very warlike air: now remember, when you see me raise up my tail, you may be sure that the battle is won, and you have then nothing to do but to rush down upon the enemy with all your force. On the other hand, if I drop my tail, the

day is lost, and you must run away as fast as you can."
Now when the gnat had heard all this, he flew back to
the tom-tit and told him every thing that had passed.

At length the day came when the battle was to be
fought; and as soon as it was light, behold! the army of
beasts came rushing forward with such a fearful sound
that the earth shook. And his majesty the tom-tit, with
his troops, came flying along in warlike array, flapping
and fluttering, and beating the air, so that it was quite
frightful to hear; and both armies set themselves in
order of battle upon the field. Now the tom-tit gave
orders to a troop of hornets that at the first onset they
should march straight towards Captain Reynard, and
fixing themselves about his tail, should sting him with
all their might and main. The hornets did as they were
told: and when Reynard felt the first sting, he started
aside and shook one of his legs, but still held up his
tail with wonderful bravery; at the second sting he was
forced to drop his tail for a moment; but when the third
hornet had fixed itself, he could bear it no longer, but
clapped his tail between his legs and scampered away
as fast as he could. As soon as the beasts saw this, they
thought of course all was lost, and scoured across the
country in the greatest dismay; leaving the birds masters
of the field.

And now the king and queen flew back in triumph
to their children, and said, "Now, children, eat, drink,
and be merry, for the victory is ours!" But the young
birds said, "No; not till Bruin has humbly begged our
pardon for calling us base-born." So the king flew back
to the bear's den, and cried out, "Thou villain bear!
come forthwith to my abode, and humbly beseech my
children to forgive thee the insult thou hast offered

them; for, if thou wilt not do this, every bone in thy wretched body shall be broken to pieces." So the bear was forced to crawl out of his den very sulkily, and do what the king bade him: and after that the young birds sat down together, and ate and drank and made merry till midnight.

# ROSE-BUD

Once upon a time there lived a king and queen who had no children; and this they lamented very much. But one day as the queen was walking by the side of the river, a little fish lifted its head out of the water, and said, "Your wish shall be fulfilled, and you shall soon have a daughter." What the little fish had foretold soon came to pass; and the queen had a little girl that was so very beautiful that the king could not cease looking on it for joy, and determined to hold a great feast. So he invited not only his relations, friends, and neighbours, but also all the fairies, that they might be kind and good to his little daughter. Now there were thirteen fairies in his kingdom, and he had only twelve golden dishes for them to eat out of, so that he was obliged to leave one of the fairies without an invitation. The rest came, and after the feast was over they gave all their best gifts to the little princess: one gave her virtue, another beauty, another riches, and so on till she had all that was excellent in the world. When eleven had done blessing her, the thirteenth, who had not been invited, and was very angry on that account, came in, and determined to take her revenge. So she cried out, "The king's daughter shall in her fifteenth year be wounded by a spindle, and fall down dead." Then the twelfth, who had not yet given her gift, came forward and said that the bad wish must be fulfilled, but that she could soften it, and that the king's daughter should not die, but fall asleep for a hundred years.

But the king hoped to save his dear child from the threatened evil, and ordered that all the spindles in the kingdom should be bought up and destroyed. All the fairies' gifts were in the mean time fulfilled; for the princess was so beautiful, and well-behaved, and amiable, and wise, that every one who knew her loved her. Now it happened that on the very day she was fifteen years old the king and queen were not at home, and she was left alone in the palace. So she roved about by herself, and looked at all the rooms and chambers, till at last she came to an old tower, to which there was a narrow staircase ending with a little door. In the door there was a golden key, and when she turned it the door sprang open, and there sat an old lady spinning away very busily. "Why, how now, good mother," said the princess, "what are you doing there?" "Spinning," said the old lady, and nodded her head. "How prettily that little thing turns round!" said the princess, and took the spindle and began to spin. But scarcely had she touched it, before the prophecy was fulfilled, and she fell down lifeless on the ground.

However, she was not dead, but had only fallen into a deep sleep; and the king and the queen, who just then came home, and all their court, fell asleep too; and the horses slept in the stables, and the dogs in the court, the pigeons on the house-top and the flies on the walls. Even the fire on the hearth left off blazing, and went to sleep; and the meat that was roasting stood still; and the cook, who was at that moment pulling the kitchen-boy by the hair to give him a box on the ear for something he had done amiss, let him go, and both fell asleep; and so every thing stood still, and slept soundly.

A large hedge of thorns soon grew round the palace, and every year it became higher and thicker, till at last the whole palace was surrounded and hid, so that not even the roof or the chimneys could be seen. But there went a report through all the land of the beautiful sleeping Rose-Bud (for so was the king's daughter called); so that from time to time several kings' sons came, and tried to break through the thicket into the palace. This they could never do; for the thorns and bushes laid hold of them as it were with hands, and there they stuck fast and died miserably.

After many many years there came a king's son into that land, and an old man told him the story of the thicket of thorns, and how a beautiful palace stood behind it, in which was a wondrous princess, called Rose-Bud, asleep with all her court. He told, too, how he had heard from his grandfather that many many princes had come, and had tried to break through the thicket, but had stuck fast and died. Then the young prince said, "All this shall not frighten me, I will go and see Rose-Bud." The old man tried to dissuade him, but he persisted in going.

Now that very day were the hundred years completed; and as the prince came to the thicket, he saw nothing but beautiful flowering shrubs, through which he passed with ease, and they closed after him as firm as ever. Then he came at last to the palace, and there in the court lay the dogs asleep, and the horses in the stables, and on

70

the roof sat the pigeons fast asleep with their heads under their wings; and when he came into the palace, the flies slept on the walls, and the cook in the kitchen was still holding up her hand as if she would beat the boy, and the maid sat with a black fowl in her hand ready to be plucked.

Then he went on still farther, and all was so still that he could hear every breath he drew; till at last he came to the old tower and opened the door of the little room in which Rose-Bud was, and there she lay fast asleep, and looked so beautiful that he could not take his eyes off, and he stooped down and gave her a kiss. But the moment he kissed her she opened her eyes and awoke, and smiled upon him. Then they went out together, and presently the king and queen also awoke, and all the court, and they gazed on each other with great wonder. And the horses got up and shook themselves, and the dogs jumped about and barked; the pigeons took their heads from under their wings, and looked about and flew into the fields; the flies on the walls buzzed away; the fire in the kitchen blazed up and cooked the dinner, and the roast meat turned round again; the cook gave the boy the box on his ear so that he cried out, and the maid went on plucking the fowl. And then was the wedding of the prince and Rose-Bud celebrated, and they lived happily together all their lives long.

# THE THREE CHILDREN OF FORTUNE

Once upon a time a father sent for his three sons, and gave to the eldest a cock, to the second a scythe, and to the third a cat. "I am now old," said he, "my end is approaching, and I would fain provide for you before I die. Money I have none, and what I now give you seems of but little worth; yet it rests with yourselves alone to turn my gifts to good account. Only seek out for a land where what you have is as yet unknown, and your fortune is made."

After the death of the father, the eldest set out with his cock: but wherever he went, in every town he saw from afar off a cock sitting upon the church steeple, and turning round with the wind. In the villages he always heard plenty of them crowing, and his bird was therefore nothing new; so there did not seem much chance of his making his fortune. At length it happened that he came to an island where the people who lived there had never heard of a cock, and knew not even how to reckon the time. They knew, indeed, if it were morning or evening; but at night, if they lay awake, they had no means of knowing how time went. "Behold," said he to them, "what a noble animal this is! how like a knight he is! he carries a bright red crest upon his head, and spurs upon his heels; he crows three times every night, at stated hours, and at the third time the sun is about to rise. But this is not all; sometimes he screams in broad day-light, and then you must take warning, for the weather is surely about to change." This pleased the

72

natives mightily; they kept awake one whole night, and heard, to their great joy, how gloriously the cock called the hour, at two, four, and six o'clock. Then they asked him whether the bird was to be sold, and how much he would sell it for. "About as much gold as an ass can carry," said he. "A very fair price for such an animal," cried they with one voice; and agreed to give him what he asked.

When he returned home with his wealth, his brothers wondered greatly; and the second said, "I will now set forth likewise, and see if I can turn my scythe to as good an account." There did not seem, however, much likelihood of this; for go where he would, he was met by peasants who had as good a scythe on their shoulders as he had. But at last, as good luck would have it, he came to an island where the people had never heard of a scythe: there, as soon as the corn was ripe, they went into the fields and pulled it up; but this was very hard work, and a great deal of it was lost. The man then set to work with his scythe; and mowed down their whole crop so quickly, that the people stood staring open-mouthed with wonder. They were willing to give him what he asked for such a marvellous thing: but he only took a horse laden with as much gold as it could carry.

Now the third brother had a great longing to go and see what he could make of his cat. So he set out: and at first it happened to him as it had to the others, so long as he kept upon the main land, he met with no success; there were plenty of cats every where, indeed too many, so that the young ones were for the most part, as soon as they came into the world, drowned in the water. At last he passed over to an island, where, as it chanced most luckily for him, nobody had ever seen a cat; and they were overrun with mice to such a degree, that the little wretches danced upon the tables and chairs, whether the master of the house were at home or not. The people complained loudly of this grievance; the king himself knew not how to rid himself of them in his palace; in every corner mice were squeaking, and they gnawed everything that their teeth could lay hold of. Here was a fine field for Puss—she soon began her chase, and had cleared two rooms in the twinkling of an eye; when the people besought their king to buy the wonderful animal, for the good of the public, at any price. The king willingly gave what was asked,—a mule laden with gold and jewels; and thus the third brother returned home with a richer prize than either of the others.

Meantime the cat feasted away upon the mice in the royal palace, and devoured so many that they were no longer in any great numbers. At length, quite spent and tired with her work, she became extremely thirsty; so she stood still, drew up her head, and cried, "Miau, Miau!" The king gathered together all his subjects when they heard this strange cry, and many ran shrieking in a great fright out of the palace. But the king held a great council below as to what was best to be done; and it was at length fixed to send a herald to the cat, to warn her to leave the castle forthwith, or that force would be used to remove her. "For," said the counsellors, "we would far more willingly put up with the mice (since we are used to that evil), than get rid of them at the risk of our lives." A page accordingly went, and asked the cat "whether she were willing to quit the castle?" But Puss, whose thirst became every moment more and more pressing, answered nothing but "Miau! Miau!" which the page

74

interpreted to mean "No! No!" and therefore carried this answer to the king. "Well," said the counsellors, "then we must try what force will do." So the guns were planted, and the palace was fired upon from all sides. When the fire reached the room where the cat was, she sprang out of the window and ran away; but the besiegers did not see her, and went on firing until the whole palace was burnt to the ground.

# FREDERICK AND CATHERINE

There was once a man called Frederick: he had a wife whose name was Catherine, and they had not long been married. One day Frederick said, "Kate! I am going to work in the fields; when I come back I shall be hungry, so let me have something nice cooked, and a good draught of ale." "Very well," said she, "it shall all be ready." When dinner-time drew nigh, Catherine took a nice steak, which was all the meat she had, and put it on the fire to fry. The steak soon began to look brown, and to crackle in the pan; and Catherine stood by with a fork and turned it: then she said to herself, "The steak is almost ready, I may as well go to the cellar for the ale." So she left the pan on the fire, and took a large jug and went into the cellar and tapped the ale cask. The beer ran into the jug, and Catherine stood looking on. At last it popped into her head, "The dog is not shut up—he may be running away with the steak; that's well thought of." So up she ran from the cellar; and sure enough the rascally cur had got the steak in his mouth, and was making off with it.

Away ran Catherine, and away ran the dog across the field! but he ran faster than she, and stuck close to the steak. "It's all gone, and 'what can't be cured must be endured,'" said Catherine. So she turned round; and as she had run a good way and was tired, she walked home leisurely to cool herself.

Now all this time the ale was running too, for Catherine had not turned the cock; and when the jug was full the liquor ran upon the floor till the cask was empty. When she got to the cellar stairs she saw what had happened. "My stars!" said she, "what shall I do to keep Frederick from seeing all this slopping about?" So she thought a while; and at last remembered that there was a sack of fine meal bought at the last fair, and that if she sprinkled this over the floor it would suck up the ale nicely. "What a lucky thing," said she, "that we kept that meal! we have now a good use for it." So away she went for it: but she managed to set it down just upon the great jug full of beer, and upset it; and thus all the ale that had been saved was set swimming on the floor also. "Ah! well," said she, "when one goes, another may as well follow." Then she strewed the meal all about the cellar, and was quite pleased with her cleverness, and said, "How very neat and clean it looks!"

At noon Frederick came home. "Now, wife," cried he, "what have you for dinner?" "O Frederick!" answered she, "I was cooking you a steak; but while I went down to draw the ale, the dog ran away with it; and while I ran after him, the ale all ran out; and when I went to dry up the ale with the sack of meal that we got at the fair, I upset the jug: but the cellar is now quite dry, and looks so clean!" "Kate, Kate," said he, "how could you do all this? Why did you leave the steak to fry, and the ale to run, and then spoil all the meal?" "Why, Frederick," said she, "I did not know I was doing wrong, you should have told me before."

The husband thought to himself, If my wife manages matters thus, I must look sharp myself. Now he had a good deal of gold in the house: so he said to Catherine, "What pretty yellow buttons these are! I shall put them into a box and bury them in the garden; but take care that you never go near or meddle with them." "No, Frederick," said she, "that I never will." As soon as he was gone, there came by some pedlars with earthenware plates and dishes, and they asked her whether she would buy. "Oh dear me, I should like to buy very much, but I have no money: if you had any use for yellow buttons, I might deal with you." "Yellow buttons!" said they: "let us have a look at them." "Go into the garden and dig where I tell you, and you will find the yellow buttons: I dare not go myself." So the rogues went: and when they found what these yellow buttons were, they took them all away, and left her plenty of plates and dishes. Then she set them all about the house for a show: and when Frederick came back, he cried out, "Kate, what have you been doing?" "See," said she, "I have bought all these with your yellow buttons: but I did not touch them myself; the pedlars went themselves and dug them up." "Wife, wife," said Frederick, "what a pretty piece of work you have made! those yellow buttons were all my money: How came you to do such a thing?" "Why," answered she, "I did not know there was any harm in it; you should have told me."

Catherine stood musing for a while, and at last said to her husband, "Hark ye, Frederick, we will soon get the gold back: let us run after the thieves." "Well, we will try," answered he; "but take some butter and cheese with you, that we may have something to eat by the way." "Very well," said she; and they set out: and as Frederick walked the fastest, he left his wife some way behind. "It does not matter," thought she: "when we turn back, I shall be so much nearer home than he."

Presently she came to the top of a hill; down the side of which there was a road so narrow that the cart-wheels always chafed the trees on each side as they passed. "Ah, see now," said she, "how they have bruised and wounded those poor trees; they will never get well." So she took pity on them, and made use of the butter to grease them all, so that the wheels might not hurt them so much. While she was doing this kind office, one of her cheeses fell out of the basket, and rolled down the hill. Catherine looked, but could not see where it was gone; so she said, "Well, I suppose the other will go the same way and find you; he has younger legs than I have." Then she rolled the other cheese after it; and away it went, nobody knows where, down the hill. But she said she supposed they knew the road, and would follow her, and she could not stay there all day waiting for them.

At last she overtook Frederick, who desired her to give him something to eat. Then she gave him the dry bread. "Where are the butter and cheese?" said he. "Oh!" answered she, "I used the butter to grease those poor trees that the wheels chafed so: and one of the cheeses ran away, so I sent the other after it to find it, and I suppose they are both on the road together somewhere." "What a goose you are to do such silly things!" said the husband. "How can you say so?" said she; "I am sure you never told me not."

They ate the dry bread together; and Frederick said, "Kate, I hope you locked the door safe when you came away." "No," answered she, "you did not tell me." "Then go home, and do it now before we go any farther," said Frederick, "and bring with you something to eat."

Catherine did as he told her, and thought to herself by the way, "Frederick wants something to eat; but I don't think he is very fond of butter and cheese: I'll bring him a bag of fine nuts, and the vinegar, for I have often seen him take some."

When she reached home, she bolted the back door, but the front door she took off the hinges, and said, "Frederick told me to lock the door, but surely it can no where be so safe as if I take it with me." So she took her time by the way: and when she overtook her husband she cried out, "There, Frederick, there is the door itself, now you may watch it as carefully as you please." "Alas! alas!" said he, "what a clever wife I have! I sent you to make the house fast, and you take the door away, so that every body may go in and out as they please:—however, as you have brought the door, you shall carry it about with you for your pains." "Very well," answered she, "I'll carry the door; but I'll not carry the nuts and vinegar bottle also,—that would be too much of a load; so, if you please, I'll fasten them to the door."

Frederick of course made no objection to that plan, and they set off into the wood to look for the thieves; but they could not find them: and when it grew dark, they climbed up into a tree to spend the night there.

Scarcely were they up, than who should come by but the very rogues they were looking for. They were in truth great rascals, and belonged to that class of people who find things before they are lost: they were tired; so they sat down and made a fire under the very tree where Frederick and Catherine were. Frederick slipped down on the other side, and picked up some stones. Then he climbed up again, and tried to hit the thieves on the head with them: but they only said, "It must be near morning, for the wind shakes the fir-apples down."

Catherine, who had the door on her shoulder, began to be very tired; but she thought it was the nuts upon it that were so heavy: so she said softly, "Frederick, I must let the nuts go." "No," answered he, "not now, they will discover us." "I can't help that, they must go." "Well then, make haste and throw them down, if you will." Then away rattled the nuts down among the boughs; and one of the thieves cried. "Bless me, it is hailing."

A little while after, Catherine thought the door was still very heavy: so she whispered to Frederick, "I must throw the vinegar down." "Pray don't," answered he, "it will discover us." "I can't help that," said she, "go it must." So she poured all the vinegar down; and the thieves said, "What a heavy dew there is!"

At last it popped into Catherine's head that it was the door itself that was so heavy all the time: so she whispered Frederick, "I must throw the door down soon." But he begged and prayed her not to do so, for he was sure it would betray them. "Here goes, however," said she: and down went the door with such a clatter upon the thieves, that they cried out "Murder!" and not knowing what was coming, ran away as fast as they could, and left all the gold. So when Frederick and Catherine came down, there they found all their money safe and sound.


# THE DOG AND THE SPARROW

A shepherd's dog had a master who took no care of him, but often let him suffer the greatest hunger. At last he could bear it no longer; so he took to his heels, and off he ran in a very sad and sorrowful mood. On the road he met a sparrow, that said to him, "Why are you so sad, my friend?" "Because," said the dog, "I am very very hungry, and have nothing to eat." "If that be all," answered the sparrow, "come with me into the next town, and I will soon find you plenty of food." So on they went together into the town: and as they passed by a butcher's shop, the sparrow said to the dog, "Stand there a little while, till I peck you down a piece of meat." So the sparrow perched upon the shelf: and having first looked carefully about her to see if any one was watching her, she pecked and scratched at a steak that lay upon the edge of the shelf, till at last down it fell. Then the dog snapped it up, and scrambled away with it into a corner, where he soon ate it all up. "Well," said the sparrow, "you shall have some more if you will; so come with me to the next shop, and I will peck you down another steak." When the dog had eaten this too, the sparrow said to him, "Well, my good friend, have you had enough now?" "I have had plenty of meat," answered he, "but I should like to have a piece of bread to eat after it." "Come with me then," said the sparrow, "and you shall soon have that too." So she took him to a baker's shop, and pecked at two rolls that lay in the window, till they fell down: and as the dog still wished for more, she took him to another shop and pecked down some more for him. When that was eaten, the sparrow asked him whether he had had enough now. "Yes," said he; "and now let us take a walk a little way out of the town." So they both went out upon the high road: but as the weather was warm, they had not gone far before the dog said, "I am very much tired,—I should like to take a nap." "Very well," answered the sparrow, "do so, and in the meantime I will perch upon that bush." So the dog stretched himself out on the road, and fell fast asleep. Whilst he slept there came by a carter with a cart drawn by three horses, and loaded with two casks of wine. The sparrow, seeing that the carter did not turn out of the way, but would go on in the track in which the dog lay, so as to drive over him, called out, "Stop! stop! Mr Carter, or it shall be the worse for you." But the carter, grumbling to himself, "You make it the worse for me, indeed! what can you do!" cracked his whip, and drove his cart over the poor dog, so that the wheels crushed him to death. "There," cried the sparrow, "thou cruel villain, thou hast killed my friend the dog. Now mind what I say. This deed of thine shall cost thee all thou art worth." "Do your worst, and welcome," said the brute, "what harm can you do me?" and passed on. But the sparrow crept under the tilt of the cart, and pecked at the bung of one of the casks till she loosened it; and then all the wine ran out, without the carter seeing it. At last he looked round, and saw that the cart was dripping, and the cask quite empty. "What an unlucky wretch I am!" cried he. "Not wretch enough yet!" said the sparrow, as she alighted upon the head of one of the horses, and pecked at him till he reared up and kicked. When the carter saw this, he drew out his hatchet and aimed a blow at the sparrow, meaning to kill her; but she flew away, and the blow fell upon the poor horse's head with such force, that he fell down dead. "Unlucky wretch that I am!" cried he. "Not wretch enough yet!" said the sparrow. And as the carter went on with the other two horses, she again crept under the tilt of the cart, and pecked out the bung of the second cask, so that all the wine ran out. When the carter saw this, he again cried out, "Miserable wretch that I am!" But the sparrow answered, "Not wretch enough yet!" and perched on the head of the second horse, and pecked at him too. The carter ran up and struck at her again with his hatchet; but away she flew, and the blow fell upon the second horse and killed him on the spot. "Unlucky wretch that I am!" said he. "Not wretch enough yet!" said the sparrow; and perching upon the third horse, she began to peck him too. The carrier was mad with fury; and without looking about him, or caring what he was about, struck again at the sparrow; but killed his third horse as he had done the other two. "Alas! miserable wretch that I am!" cried he. "Not wretch enough yet!" answered the sparrow as she flew away; "now will I plague and punish thee at thy own house." The carter was forced at last to leave his cart behind him, and to go home overflowing with rage and vexation. "Alas!" said he to his wife, "what ill luck has befallen me!—my wine is all spilt, and my horses all three dead." "Alas! husband," replied she, "and a wicked bird has come into the house, and has brought with her all the birds in the world, I am sure, and they have fallen upon our corn in the loft, and are eating it up at such a rate!" Away ran the husband up stairs, and saw thousands of birds sitting upon the floor eating up his corn, with the sparrow in the midst of them. "Unlucky wretch that I am!" cried the carter; for he saw that the corn was almost all gone. "Not wretch enough yet!" said the sparrow; "thy cruelty shall cost thee thy life yet!" and away she flew.

The carter seeing that he had thus lost all that he had, went down into his kitchen; and was still not sorry for what he had done, but sat himself angrily and sulkily in the chimney corner. But the sparrow sat on the outside of the window, and cried "Carter! thy cruelty shall cost thee thy life!" With that he jumped up in a rage, seized his hatchet, and threw it at the sparrow; but it missed her, and only broke the window. The sparrow now hopped in, perched upon the window-seat, and cried, "Carter! it shall cost thee thy life!" Then he became mad and blind with rage, and struck the window seat with such force that he cleft it in two: and as the sparrow flew from place to place, the carter and his wife were so furious, that they broke all their furniture, glasses, chairs, benches, the table, and at last the walls, without touching the bird at all. In the end, however, they caught her: and the wife said, "Shall I kill her at once?" "No," cried he, "that is letting her off too easily: she shall die a much more cruel death; I will eat her." But the sparrow began to flutter about, and stretched out her neck and cried, "Carter! it shall cost thee thy life yet!" With that he could wait no longer: so he gave his wife the hatchet, and cried, "Wife, strike at the bird and kill her in my hand." And the wife struck; but she missed her aim, and hit her husband on the head so that he fell down dead, and the sparrow flew quietly home to her nest.

## THE QUEEN BEE

Two king's sons once upon a time went out into the world to seek their fortunes; but they soon fell into a wasteful foolish way of living, so that they could not return home again. Then their young brother, who was a little insignificant dwarf, went out to seek for his brothers: but when he had found them they only laughed at him, to think that he, who was so young and simple, should try to travel through the world, when they, who were so much wiser, had been unable to get on. However, they all set out on their journey together, and came at last to an ant-hill. The two elder brothers would have pulled it down, in order to see how the poor ants in their fright would run about and carry off their eggs. But the little dwarf said, "Let the poor things enjoy themselves, I will not suffer you to trouble them."

So on they went, and came to a lake where many many ducks were swimming about. The two brothers wanted to catch two, and roast them. But the dwarf said, "Let the poor things enjoy themselves, you shall not kill them." Next they came to a bees' nest in a hollow tree, and there was so much honey that it ran down the trunk; and the two brothers wanted to light a fire under the tree and kill the bees, so as to get their honey. But the dwarf held them back, and said, "Let the pretty insects enjoy themselves, I cannot let you burn them."

At length the three brothers came to a castle: and as they passed by the stables they saw fine horses standing there, but all were of marble, and no man was to be seen. Then they went through all the rooms, till they came to a door on which were three locks: but in the middle of the door there was a wicket, so that they could look into the next room. There they saw a little grey old man sitting at a table; and they called to him once or twice, but he did not hear: however, they called a third time, and then he rose and came out to them.

He said nothing, but took hold of them and led them to a beautiful table covered with all sorts of good things: and when they had eaten and drunk, he showed each of them to a bedchamber.

The next morning he came to the eldest and took him to a marble table, where were three tablets, containing an account of the means by which the castle might be disenchanted. The first tablet said—"In the wood, under the moss, lie the thousand pearls belonging to the king's daughter; they must all be found: and if one be missing by set of sun, he who seeks them will be turned into marble."

The eldest brother set out, and sought for the pearls the whole day; but the evening came, and he had not found the first hundred: so he was turned into stone as the tablet had foretold.

The next day the second brother undertook the task; but he succeeded no better than the first; for he could only find the second hundred of the pearls; and therefore he too was turned into stone.

At last came the little dwarf's turn: and he looked in the moss; but it was so hard to find the pearls, and the job was so tiresome!—so he sat down upon a stone and cried. And as he sat there, the king of the ants (whose life he had saved) came to help him, with five thousand ants; and it was not long before they had found all the pearls and laid them in a heap.

The second tablet said—"The key of the princess's bed-chamber must be fished up out of the lake." And as the dwarf came to the brink of it, he saw the two ducks whose lives he had saved swimming about; and they dived down and soon brought up the key from the bottom.

The third task was the hardest. It was to choose out the youngest and the best of the king's three daughters. Now they were all beautiful, and all exactly alike: but he was told that the eldest had eaten a piece of sugar, the next some sweet syrup, and the youngest a spoonful of honey; so he was to guess which it was that had eaten the honey.

Then came the queen of the bees, who had been saved by the little dwarf from the fire, and she tried the lips of all three; but at last she sat upon the lips of the one that had eaten the honey; and so the dwarf knew which was the youngest. Thus the spell was broken, and all who had been turned into stones awoke, and took their proper forms. And the dwarf married the youngest and the best of the princesses, and was king after her father's death; but his two brothers married the other two sisters.

# THE WONDERFUL MUSICIAN

There was once a capital musician who played delightfully on the fiddle, and he went rambling in a forest in a merry mood. Then he said to himself, "Time goes rather heavily on, I must find a companion." So he took up his fiddle, and fiddled away till the wood resounded with his music.

Presently up came a wolf. "Dear me! there's a wolf coming to see me," said the musician. But the wolf came up to him, and said, "How very prettily you play! I wish you would teach me." "That is easily done," said the musician, "if you will only do what I bid you." "Yes," replied the wolf, "I shall be a very apt scholar." So they went on a little way together, and came at last to an old oak tree that was hollow within, and had a large crack in the middle of the trunk. "Look there," said the musician, "if you wish to learn to fiddle, put your fore feet into that crack." The wolf did as he was bid: but the musician picked up a large stone and wedged both his forefeet fast into the crack, so as to make him a prisoner. "Now be so good as to wait there till I come back," said he, and jogged on.

After a while, he said again to himself, "Time goes very heavily, I must find another companion." So he took his fiddle, and fiddled away again in the wood. Presently up came a fox that was wandering close by. "Ah! there is a fox," said he. The fox came up and said, "You delightful musician, how prettily you play! I must and will learn to play as you do." "That you may soon do," said the musician, "if you do as I tell you." "That I will," said the fox. So they travelled on together till they came to a narrow footpath with high bushes on each side. Then the musician bent a stout hazel stem down to the ground from one side of the path, and set his foot on the top, and held it fast; and bent another from the other side, and said to the fox, "Now, pretty fox, if you want to fiddle, give me hold of your left paw." So the fox gave him his paw; and he tied it fast to the top of one of the hazel stems. "Now give me your right," said he; and the fox did as he was told: then the musician tied that paw to the other hazel; and took off his foot, and away up flew the bushes, and the fox too, and hung sprawling and swinging in the air. "Now be so kind as to stay there till I come back," said the musician, and jogged on.

But he soon said to himself, "Time begins to hang heavy, I must find a companion." So he took up his fiddle and fiddled away divinely. Then up came a hare running along. "Ah! there is a hare," said the musician. And the hare said to him, "You fine fiddler, how beautifully you play! will you teach me?" "Yes," said the musician, "I will soon do that, if you will follow my orders." "Yes," said the hare, "I shall make a good scholar." Then they went on together very well for a long while, till they came to an open space in the wood. The musician tied a string round the hare's neck, and fastened the other end to the tree. "Now," said he, "pretty hare, quick, jump about, run round the tree twenty times." So the silly hare did as she was bid: and when she had run twenty times round the tree, she had twisted the string twenty times round the trunk, and was fast prisoner; and she might pull and pull away as long as she pleased, and only pulled the string faster about her neck. "Now wait there till I come back," said the musician.

But the wolf had pulled and bitten and scratched at the stone a long while, till at last he had got his feet out and was at liberty. Then he said in a great passion, "I will run after that rascally musician and tear him in pieces." As the fox saw him run by, he said, "Ah, brother wolf, pray let me down, the musician has played tricks with me." So the wolf set to work at the bottom of the hazel stem, and bit it in two; and away went both together to find the musician: and as they came to the hare, she cried out too for help. So they went and set her free, and all followed the enemy together.

Meantime the musician had been fiddling away, and found another companion; for a poor woodcutter had been pleased with the music, and could not help following him with his axe under his arm. The musician was pleased to get a man for his companion, and behaved very civilly to him, and played him no tricks, but stopped and played his prettiest tunes till his heart overflowed for joy. While the woodcutter was standing listening, he saw the wolf, the fox, and the hare coming, and knew by their faces that they were in a great rage, and coming to do some mischief. So he stood before the musician with his great axe, as much as to say, No one shall hurt him as long as I have this axe. And when the beasts saw this, they were so frightened that they ran back into the wood. Then the musician played the woodcutter one of his best tunes for his pains, and went on with his journey.

# JORINDA AND JORINDEL

There was once an old castle that stood in the middle of a large thick wood, and in the castle lived an old fairy. All the day long she flew about in the form of an owl, or crept about the country like a cat; but at night she always became an old woman again. When any youth came within a hundred paces of her castle, he became quite fixed, and could not move a step till she came and set him free: but when any pretty maiden came within that distance, she was changed into a bird; and the fairy put her into a cage and hung her up in a chamber in the castle. There were seven hundred of these cages hanging in the castle, and all with beautiful birds in them.

Now there was once a maiden whose name was Jorinda: she was prettier than all the pretty girls that ever were seen; and a shepherd whose name was Jorindel was very fond of her, and they were soon to be married. One day they went to walk in the wood, that they might be alone: and Jorindel said, "We must take care that we don't go too near to the castle." It was a beautiful evening; the last rays of the setting sun shone bright through the long stems of the trees upon the green underwood beneath, and the turtledoves sang plaintively from the tall birches.

Jorinda sat down to gaze upon the sun; Jorindel sat by her side; and both felt sad, they knew not why; but it seemed as if they were to be parted from one another for ever. They had wandered a long way; and when they looked to see which way they should go home, they found themselves at a loss to know what path to take.

The sun was setting fast, and already half of his circle had disappeared behind the hill: Jorindel on a sudden looked behind him, and as he saw through the bushes that they had, without knowing it, sat down close under the old walls of the castle, he shrank for fear, turned pale, and trembled. Jorinda was singing,

> "The ring-dove sang from the willow spray,
>     Well-a-day! well-a-day!
> He mourn'd for the fate
> Of his lovely mate,
>     Well-a-day!"

The song ceased suddenly. Jorindel turned to see the reason, and beheld his Jorinda changed into a nightingale; so that her song ended with a mournful *jug, jug*. An owl with fiery eyes flew three times round them, and three times screamed *Tu whu! Tu whu! Tu whu!* Jorindel could not move: he stood fixed as a stone, and could neither weep, nor speak, nor stir hand or foot. And now the sun went quite down; the gloomy night came; the owl flew into a bush; and a moment after the old fairy came forth, pale and meagre, with staring eyes, and a nose and chin that almost met one another.

She mumbled something to herself, seized the nightingale, and went away with it in her hand. Poor Jorindel saw the nightingale was gone,—but what could he do? he could not move from the spot where he stood. At last the fairy came back, and sung with a hoarse voice,

"Till the prisoner's fast,
And her doom is cast,
    There stay! Oh, stay!
When the charm is around her,
And the spell has bound her,
    Hie away! away!"

On a sudden Jorindel found himself free. Then he fell on his knees before the fairy, and prayed her to give him back his dear Jorinda: but she said he should never see her again, and went her way.

He prayed, he wept, he sorrowed, but all in vain. "Alas!" he said, "what will become of me?"

He could not return to his own home, so he went to a strange village, and employed himself in keeping sheep. Many a time did he walk round and round as near to the hated castle as he dared go. At last he dreamt one night that he found a beautiful purple flower, and in the middle of it lay a costly pearl; and he dreamt that he plucked the flower, and went with it in his hand into the castle, and that every thing he touched with it was disenchanted, and that there he found his dear Jorinda again.

In the morning when he awoke, he began to search over hill and dale for this pretty flower; and eight long days he sought for it in vain: but on the ninth day early in the morning he found the beautiful purple flower; and in the middle of it was a large dew drop as big as a costly pearl.

Then he plucked the flower, and set out and travelled day and night till he came again to the castle. He walked nearer than a hundred paces to it, and yet he did not become fixed as before, but found that he could go close up to the door.

Jorindel was very glad to see this: he touched the door with the flower, and it sprang open, so that he went in through the court, and listened when he heard so many birds singing. At last he came to the chamber where the fairy sat, with the seven hundred birds singing in the seven hundred cages. And when she saw Jorindel she was very angry, and screamed with rage; but she could not come within two yards of him; for the flower he held in his hand protected him. He looked around at the birds, but alas! there were many many nightingales, and how then should he find his Jorinda? While he was thinking what to do, he observed that the fairy had taken down one of the cages, and was making her escape through the door. He ran or flew to her, touched the cage with the flower,—and his Jorinda stood before him. She threw her arms round his neck and looked as beautiful as ever, as beautiful as when they walked together in the wood.

Then he touched all the other birds with the flower, so that they resumed their old forms; and took his dear Jorinda home, where they lived happily together many years.


# THE GRATEFUL BEASTS


A certain man, who had lost almost all his money, resolved to set off with the little that was left him, and travel into the wide world. Then the first place he came to was a village, where the young people were running about crying and shouting. "What is the matter?" asked he. "See here," answered they, "we have got a mouse that we make dance to please us. Do look at him: what a droll sight it is! how he jumps about!" But the man pitied the poor little thing, and said, "Let the mouse go, and I will give you money." So he gave them some, and took the mouse and let him run; and he soon jumped into a hole that was close by, and was out of their reach.

Then he travelled on and came to another village, and there the children had got an ass that they made stand on its hind legs and tumble, at which they laughed and shouted, and gave the poor beast no rest. So the good man gave them also some money to let the poor ass alone.

At the next village he came to, the young people had got a bear that had been taught to dance, and they were plaguing the poor thing sadly. Then he gave them too some money to let the beast go, and the bear was very glad to get on his four feet, and seemed quite happy.

But the man had now given away all the money he had in the world, and had not a shilling in his pocket. Then said he to himself, "The king has heaps of gold in his treasury that he never uses; I cannot die of hunger, I hope I shall be forgiven if I borrow a little, and when I get rich again I will repay it all."

Then he managed to get into the treasury, and took a very little money; but as he came out the king's guards saw him; so they said he was a thief, and took him to the Judge, and he was sentenced to be thrown into the water in a box. The lid of the box was full of holes to let in air, and a jug of water and a loaf of bread were given him.

Whilst he was swimming along in the water very sorrowfully, he heard something nibbling and biting at the lock; and all of a sudden it fell off, the lid flew open, and there stood his old friend the little mouse, who had done him this service. And then came the ass and the bear, and pulled the box ashore; and all helped him because he had been kind to them.

But now they did not know what to do next, and began to consult together; when on a sudden a wave threw on the shore a beautiful white stone that looked like an egg. Then the bear said, "That's a lucky thing: this is the wonderful stone, and whoever has it may have every thing else that he wishes." So the man went and picked up the stone, and wished for a palace and a garden, and a stud of horses; and his wish was fulfilled as soon as he had made it. And there he lived in his castle and garden, with fine stables and horses; and all was so grand and beautiful, that he never could wonder and gaze at it enough.

After some time, some merchants passed by that way. "See," said they, "what a princely palace! The last time we were here, it was nothing but a desert waste." They were very curious to know how all this had happened; so they went in and asked the master of the palace how it had been so quickly raised. "I have done nothing myself," answered he, "it is the wonderful stone that did all."—"What a strange stone that must be!" said they: then he invited them in and showed it to them. They asked him whether he would sell it, and offered him all their goods for it; and the goods seemed so fine and costly, that he quite forgot that the stone would bring him in a moment a thousand better and richer things, and he agreed to make the bargain.

Scarcely was the stone, however, out of his hands before all his riches were gone, and he found himself sitting in his box in the water, with his jug of water and loaf of bread by his side. The grateful beasts, the mouse, the ass, and the bear, came directly to help him; but the mouse found she could not nibble off the lock this time, for it was a great deal stronger than before. Then the bear said, "We must find the wonderful stone again, or all our endeavours will be fruitless."

The merchants, meantime, had taken up their abode in the palace; so away went the three friends, and when they came near, the bear said, "Mouse, go in and look through the key-hole and see where the stone is kept: you are small, nobody will see you." The mouse did as she was told, but soon came back and said, "Bad news! I have looked in, and the stone hangs under the looking-glass by a red silk string, and on each side of it sits a great cat with fiery eyes to watch it."

Then the others took council together and said, "Go back again, and wait till the master of the palace is in bed asleep, then nip his nose and pull his hair." Away went the mouse, and did as they directed her; and the master jumped up very angry, and rubbed his nose, and cried, "Those rascally cats are good for nothing at all, they let the mice eat my very nose and pull the hair off my head." Then he hunted them out of the room; and so the mouse had the best of the game.

Next night as soon as the master was asleep, the mouse crept in again, and nibbled at the red silk string to which the stone hung, till down it dropped, and she rolled it along to the door; but when it got there, the poor little mouse was quite tired; so she said to the ass, "Put in your foot, and lift it over the threshold." This was soon done: and they took up the stone, and set off for the water side. Then the ass said, "How shall we reach the box?" But the bear answered, "That is easily managed; I can swim very well, and do you, donkey, put your fore feet over my shoulders;—mind and hold fast, and take the stone in your mouth: as for you, mouse, you can sit in my ear."

It was all settled thus, and away they swam. After a time, the bear began to brag and boast: "We are brave fellows, are not we, ass?" said he; "what do you think?" But the ass held his tongue, and said not a word. "Why don't you answer me?" said the bear, "you must be an ill-mannered brute not to speak when you're spoken to." When the ass heard this, he could hold no longer; so he opened his mouth, and dropped the wonderful stone. "I could not speak," said he; "did not you know I had the stone in my mouth? now 'tis lost, and that's your fault." "Do but hold your tongue and be quiet," said the bear; "and let us think what's to be done."

Then a council was held: and at last they called together all the frogs, their wives and families, relations and friends, and said: "A great enemy is coming to eat you all up; but never mind, bring us up plenty of stones, and we'll build a strong wall to guard you." The frogs hearing this were dreadfully frightened, and set to work, bringing up all the stones they could find. At last came a large fat frog pulling along the wonderful stone by the silken string: and when the bear saw it, he jumped for joy, and said, "Now we have found what we wanted." So he released the old frog from his load, and told him to tell his friends they might go about their business as soon as they pleased.

Then the three friends swam off again for the box; and the lid flew open, and they found that they were but just in time, for the bread was all eaten, and the jug almost empty. But as soon as the good man had the stone in his hand, he wished himself safe and sound in his palace again; and in a moment there he was, with his garden and his stables and his horses; and his three faithful friends dwelt with him, and they all spent their time happily and merrily as long as they lived.

# SNOW-DROP

It was in the middle of winter, when the broad flakes of snow were falling around, that a certain queen sat working at a window, the frame of which was made of fine black ebony; and as she was looking out upon the snow, she pricked her finger, and three drops of blood fell upon it. Then she gazed thoughtfully upon the red drops which sprinkled the white snow, and said, "Would that my little daughter may be as white as that snow, as red as the blood, and as black as the ebony window-frame!" And so the little girl grew up: her skin was as white as snow, her cheeks as rosy as the blood, and her hair as black as ebony; and she was called Snow-drop.

But this queen died; and the king soon married another wife, who was very beautiful, but so proud that she could not bear to think that any one could surpass her. She had a magical looking-glass, to which she used to go and gaze upon herself in it, and say,

"Tell me, glass, tell me true!
  Of all the ladies in the land,
Who is the fairest? tell me who?"

And the glass answered,

"Thou, queen, art fairest in the land."

But Snow-drop grew more and more beautiful; and when she was seven years old, she was as bright as the day, and fairer than the queen herself. Then the glass one day answered the queen, when she went to consult it as usual,

"Thou, queen, may'st fair and beauteous be,
But Snow-drop is lovelier far than thee!"

When she heard this, she turned pale with rage and envy; and called to one of her servants and said, "Take Snow-drop away into the wide wood, that I may never see her more." Then the servant led her away; but his heart melted when she begged him to spare her life, and he said, "I will not hurt thee, thou pretty child." So he left her by herself; and though he thought it most likely that the wild beasts would tear her in pieces, he felt as if a great weight were taken off his heart when he had made up his mind not to kill her, but leave her to her fate.

Then poor Snow-drop wandered along through the wood in great fear; and the wild beasts roared about her, but none did her any harm. In the evening she came to a little cottage, and went in there to rest herself, for her little feet would carry her no farther. Every thing was spruce and neat in the cottage: on the table was spread a white cloth, and there were seven little plates with seven little loaves, and seven little glasses with wine in them; and knives and forks laid in order; and by the wall stood seven little beds. Then, as she was very hungry, she picked a little piece off each loaf, and drank a very little wine out of each glass; and after that she thought she would lie down and rest. So she tried all the little beds; and one was too long, and another was too short, till at last the seventh suited her; and there she laid herself down, and went to sleep.

Presently in came the masters of the cottage, who were seven little dwarfs that lived among the mountains, and dug and searched for gold. They lighted up their seven lamps, and saw directly that all was not right. The first said, "Who has been sitting on my stool?" The second, "Who has been eating off my plate?" The third, "Who has been picking my bread?" The fourth, "Who has been meddling with my spoon?" The fifth, "Who has been handling my fork?" The sixth, "Who has been cutting with my knife?" The seventh, "Who has been drinking my wine?" Then the first looked round and said, "Who has been lying on my bed?" And the rest came running to him, and every one cried out that somebody had been upon his bed. But the seventh saw Snow-drop, and called all his brethren to come and see her; and they cried out with wonder and astonishment, and brought their lamps to look at her, and said, "Good heavens! what a lovely child she is!" And they were delighted to see her, and took care not to wake her; and the seventh dwarf slept an hour with each of the other dwarfs in turn, till the night was gone.

In the morning, Snow-drop told them all her story; and they pitied her, and said if she would keep all things in order, and cook and wash, and knit and spin for them, she might stay where she was, and they would take good care of her. Then they went out all day long to their work, seeking for gold and silver in the mountains; and Snow-drop remained at home: and they warned her, and said, "The queen will soon find out where you are, so take care and let no one in."

But the queen, now that she thought Snow-drop was dead, believed that she was certainly the handsomest lady in the land; and she went to her glass and said,

"Tell me, glass, tell me true!
    Of all the ladies in the land,
Who is the fairest? tell me who?"

And the glass answered,

'Thou, queen, art the fairest in all this land;
But over the hills, in the greenwood shade,
Where the seven dwarfs their dwelling have made,
There Snow-drop is hiding her head, and she
Is lovelier far, O queen! than thee."

Then the queen was very much alarmed; for she knew that the glass always spoke the truth, and was sure that the servant had betrayed her. And she could not bear to think that any one lived who was more beautiful than she was; so she disguised herself as an old pedlar, and went her way over the hills to the place where the dwarfs dwelt. Then she knocked at the door, and cried "Fine wares to sell!" Snowdrop looked out at the window, and said, "Good-day, good-woman; what have you to sell?" "Good wares, fine wares," said she; "laces and bobbins of all colours." "I will let the old lady in; she seems to be a very good sort of body," thought Snow-drop; so she ran down, and unbolted the door. "Bless me!" said the old woman, "how badly your stays are laced! Let me lace them up with one of my nice new laces." Snow-drop did not dream of any mischief; so she stood up before the old woman; but she set to work so nimbly, and pulled the lace so tight, that Snow-drop lost her breath, and fell down as if she were dead. "There's an end of all thy beauty," said the spiteful queen, and went away home.

In the evening the seven dwarfs returned; and I need not saw how grieved they were to see their faithful Snow-drop stretched upon the ground motionless, as if she were quite dead. However, they lifted her up, and when they found what was the matter, they cut the lace; and in a little time she began to breathe, and soon came to life again. Then they said, "The old woman was the queen herself; take care another time, and let no one in when we are away."

When the queen got home, she went straight to her glass, and spoke to it as usual; but to her great surprise it still said,

"Thou, queen, art the fairest in all this land;
But over the hills, in the greenwood shade,
Where the seven dwarfs their dwelling have made,
There Snow-drop is hiding her head; and she
Is lovelier far, O queen! than thee."

Then the blood ran cold in her heart with spite and malice to see that Snow-drop still lived; and she dressed herself up again in a disguise, but very different from the one she wore before, and took with her a poisoned comb. When she reached the dwarfs' cottage, she knocked at the door, and cried "Fine wares to sell!" But Snow-drop said, "I dare not let any one in." Then the queen said, "Only look at my beautiful combs;" and gave her the poisoned one. And it looked so pretty that she took it up and put it into her hair to try it; but the moment it touched her head the poison was so powerful that she fell down senseless. "There you may lie," said the queen, and went her way. But by good luck the dwarfs returned very early that evening; and when they saw Snow-drop lying on the ground, they thought what had happened, and soon found the poisoned comb. And when they took it away, she recovered, and told them all that had passed; and they warned her once more not to open the door to any one.

Meantime the queen went home to her glass, and trembled with rage when she received exactly the same answer as before; and she said, "Snow-drop shall die, if it costs me my life." So she went secretly into a chamber, and prepared a poisoned apple: the outside looked very rosy and tempting, but whoever tasted it was sure to die. Then she dressed herself up as a peasant's wife, and travelled over the hills to the dwarfs' cottage, and knocked at the door; but Snow-drop put her head out of the window and said, "I dare not let any one in, for the dwarfs have told me not." "Do as you please," said the old woman, "but at any rate take this pretty apple; I will make you a present of it." "No," said Snow-drop, "I dare not take it." "You silly girl!" answered the other, "what are you afraid of? do you think it is poisoned? Come! do you eat one part, and I will eat the other." Now the apple was so prepared that one side was good, though the other side was poisoned. Then Snow-drop was very much tempted to taste, for the apple looked exceedingly nice; and when she saw the old woman eat, she could refrain no longer. But she had scarcely put the piece into her mouth, when she fell down dead upon the ground. "This time nothing will save thee," said the queen; and she went home to her glass, and at last it said

"Thou, queen, art the fairest of all the fair."

And then her envious heart was glad, and as happy as such a heart could be.

When evening came, and the dwarfs returned home, they found Snow-drop lying on the ground: no breath passed her lips, and they were afraid that she was quite dead. They lifted her up, and combed her hair, and washed her face with wine and water; but all was in vain, for the little girl seemed quite dead. So they laid her down upon a bier, and all seven watched and bewailed her three whole days; and then they proposed to bury her: but her cheeks were still rosy, and her face looked just as it did while she was alive; so they said, "We will never bury her in the cold ground." And they made a coffin of glass, so that they might still look at her, and wrote her name upon it, in golden letters, and that she was a king's daughter. And the coffin was placed upon the hill, and one of the dwarfs always sat by it and watched. And the birds of the air came too, and bemoaned Snow-drop: first of all came an owl, and then a raven, but at last came a dove.

And thus Snow-drop lay for a long long time, and still only looked as though she were asleep; for she was even now as white as snow, and as red as blood, and as black as ebony. At last a prince came and called at the dwarfs' house; and he saw Snow-drop, and read what was written in golden letters. Then he offered the dwarfs money, and earnestly prayed them to let him take her

away; but they said, "We will not part with her for all
the gold in the world." At last however they had pity on
him, and gave him the coffin: but the moment he lifted
it up to carry it home with him, the piece of apple fell
from between her lips, and Snow-drop awoke, and said,
"Where am I?" And the prince answered, "Thou art safe
with me." Then he told her all that had happened, and
said, "I love you better than all the world: come with
me to my father's palace, and you shall be my wife."
And Snow-drop consented, and went home with the
prince; and every thing was prepared with great pomp
and splendour for their wedding.

To the feast was invited, among the rest, Snow-drop's
old enemy the queen; and as she was dressing herself
in fine rich clothes, she looked in the glass, and said,

> "Tell me, glass, tell me true!
> Of all the ladies in the land,
> Who is fairest? tell me who?"

And the glass answered,

> "Thou, lady, art loveliest *here*, I ween;
> But lovelier far is the new-made queen."

When she heard this, she started with rage; but her
envy and curiosity were so great, that she could not help
setting out to see the bride. And when she arrived, and
saw that it was no other than Snow-drop, who, as she
thought, had been dead a long while, she choked with
passion, and fell ill and died; but Snow-drop and the
prince lived and reigned happily over that land many
many years.

# THE ADVENTURES OF CHANTICLEER AND PARTLET

## 1. How they went to the Mountains to eat Nuts

"The nuts are quite ripe now," said Chanticleer to his wife Partlet, "suppose we go together to the mountains, and eat as many as we can, before the squirrel takes them all away." "With all my heart," said Partlet, "let us go and make a holiday of it together." So they went to the mountains; and as it was a lovely day they stayed there till the evening. Now, whether it was that they had eaten so many nuts that they could not walk, or whether they were lazy and would not, I do not know: however, they took it into their heads that it did not become them to go home on foot. So Chanticleer began to build a little carriage of nut-shells: and when it was finished, Partlet jumped into it and sat down, and bid Chanticleer harness himself to it and draw her home. "That's a good joke!" said Chanticleer; "no, that will never do; I had rather by half walk home; I'll sit on the box and be coachman, if you like, but I'll not draw." While this was passing, a duck came quacking up, and cried out, "You thieving vagabonds, what business have you in my grounds; I'll give it you well for your insolence!" and upon that she fell upon Chanticleer most lustily. But Chanticleer was no coward, and returned the duck's blows with his sharp spurs so fiercely, that she soon began to cry out for mercy; which was only granted her upon condition that she would draw the carriage home for them. This she agreed to do; and Chanticleer got upon the box, and drove, crying. "Now, duck, get on as fast as you can." And away they went at a pretty good pace.

After they had travelled along a little way, they met a needle and a pin walking together along the road: and the needle cried out, "Stop! stop!" and said it was so dark that they could hardly find their way, and such dirty walking they could not get on at all: he told them that he and his friend, the pin, had been at a public house a few miles off, and had sat drinking till they had forgotten how late it was; he begged therefore that the travellers would be so kind as to give them a lift in their carriage. Chanticleer, observing that they were but thin fellows, and not likely to take up much room, told them they might ride, but made them promise not to dirty the wheels of the carriage in getting in, nor to tread on Partlet's toes.

Late at night they arrived at an inn; and as it was bad travelling in the dark, and the duck seemed much tired, and waddled about a good deal from one side to the other, they made up their minds to fix their quarters there: but the landlord at first was unwilling, and said his house was full, thinking they might not be very respectable company: however, they spoke civilly to him, and gave him the egg which Partlet had laid by the way, and said they would give him the duck, who was in the habit of laying one every day: so at last he let them come in, and they bespoke a handsome supper, and spent the evening very jollily.

Early in the morning, before it was quite light, and when no body was stirring in the inn, Chanticleer awakened his wife, and, fetching the egg, they pecked a hole in it, ate it up, and threw the shells into the fire-place: they then went to the pin and needle, who were fast asleep, and, seizing them by their heads, stuck one into the landlord's easy chair, and the other into his handkerchief; and having done this, they crept away as softly as possible. However, the duck, who slept in the open air in the yard, heard them coming, and jumping into the brook which ran close by the inn, soon swam out of their reach.

An hour or two afterwards the landlord got up, and took his handkerchief to wipe his face, but the pin ran into him and pricked him: then he walked into the kitchen to light his pipe at the fire, but when he stirred it up the egg-shells flew into his eyes, and almost blinded him. "Bless me!" said he, "all the world seems to have a design against my head this morning:" and so saying, he threw himself sulkily into his easy chair; but, oh dear! the needle ran into him; and this time the pain was not in his head. He now flew into a very great passion, and, suspecting the company who had come in the night before, he went to look after them, but they were all off; so he swore that he never again would take in such a troop of vagabonds, who ate a great deal, paid no reckoning, and gave him nothing for his trouble but their apish tricks.

## 2. How Chanticleer and Partlet went to visit Mr Korbes

Another day, Chanticleer and Partlet wished to ride out together; so Chanticleer built a handsome carriage with four red wheels, and harnessed six mice to it; and then he and Partlet got into the carriage, and away they drove. Soon afterwards a cat met them,

and said, "Where are you going?" And Chanticleer
replied,

> "All on our way
> A visit to pay
> To Mr Korbes, the fox, today."

Then the cat said, "Take me with you." Chanticleer
said, "With all my heart: get up behind, and be sure
you do not fall off."

> "Take care of this handsome coach of mine,
> Nor dirty my pretty red wheels so fine!
>   Now, mice, be ready,
>   And, wheels, run steady!
> For we are going a visit to pay
> To Mr Korbes, the fox, today."

Soon after came up a mill-stone, an egg, a duck, and
a pin; and Chanticleer gave them all leave to get into
the carriage and go with them.

When they arrived at Mr Korbes's house, he was
not at home; so the mice drew the carriage into the
coach-house, Chanticleer and Partlet flew upon a beam,
the cat sat down in the fire-place, the duck got into
the washing cistern, the pin stuck himself into the bed
pillow, the mill-stone laid himself over the house door,
and the egg rolled herself up in the towel.

When Mr Korbes came home he went to the fire-place
to make a fire; but the cat threw all the ashes in his eyes:
so he ran to the kitchen to wash himself; but there the
duck splashed all the water in his face; and when he
tried to wipe himself, the egg broke to pieces in the

towel all over his face and eyes. Then he was very angry, and went without his supper to bed; but when he laid his head on the pillow the pin ran into his cheek: at this he became quite furious, and, jumping up, would have run out of the house; but when he came to the door the mill-stone fell down on his head and killed him on the spot.

### 3. How Partlet died and was buried and how Chanticleer died of grief

Another day Chanticleer and Partlet agreed to go again to the mountains to eat nuts; and it was settled that all the nuts which they found should be shared equally between them. Now Partlet found a very large nut; but she said nothing about it to Chanticleer, and kept it all to herself: however, it was so big that she could not swallow it, and it stuck in her throat. Then she was in a great fright, and cried out to Chanticleer, "Pray run as fast as you can, and fetch me some water, or I shall be choked." Chanticleer ran as fast as he could to the river, and said, "River, give me some water, for Partlet lies on the mountain, and will be choked by a great nut." The river said, "Run first to the bride, and ask her for a silken cord to draw up the water." Chanticleer ran to the bride, and said, "Bride, you must give me a silken cord, for then the river will give me water, and the water I will carry to Partlet, who lies on the mountain, and will be choked by a great nut." But the bride said, "Run first and bring me my garland that is hanging on a willow in the garden." Then Chanticleer ran to the garden, and took the garland from the bough where it hung, and brought it to the bride; and then the bride gave him the silken cord, and he took the silken cord to the river, and the river gave him water, and he carried the water to Partlet; but in the mean time she was choked by the great nut, and lay quite dead, and never moved any more.

Then Chanticleer was very sorry, and cried bitterly; and all the beasts came and wept with him over poor Partlet. And six mice built a little hearse to carry her to her grave; and when it was ready they harnessed themselves before it, and Chanticleer drove them. On the way they met the fox. "Where are you going, Chanticleer?" said he. "To bury my Partlet," said the other, "May I go with you?" said the fox. "Yes; but you must get up behind, or my horses will not be able to draw you." Then the fox got up behind; and presently the wolf, the bear, the goat, and all the beasts of the wood, came and climbed upon the hearse.

So on they went till they came to a rapid stream. "How shall we get over?" said Chanticleer. Then said a straw, "I will lay myself across, and you may pass over upon me." But as the mice were going over, the straw slipped away and fell into the water, and the six mice all fell in and were drowned. What was to be done? Then a large log of wood came and said, "I am big enough; I will lay myself across the stream, and you shall pass over upon me." So he laid himself down; but they managed so clumsily, that the log of wood fell in and was carried away by the stream. Then a stone, who saw what had happened, came up and kindly offered to help poor Chanticleer by laying himself across the stream; and this time he got safely to the other side with the hearse, and managed to get Partlet out of it; but the fox and the other mourners, who were sitting behind, were too heavy, and fell back into the water and were all carried away by the stream, and drowned.

Thus Chanticleer was left alone with his dead Partlet; and having dug a grave for her, he laid her in it, and made a little hillock over her. Then he sat down by the grave, and wept and mourned, till at last he died too: and so all were dead.

# THE MISER IN THE BUSH

A farmer had a faithful and diligent servant, who had worked hard for him three years, without having been paid any wages. At last it came into the man's head that he would not go on thus without pay any longer; so he went to his master, and said, "I have worked hard for you a long time, I will trust to you to give me what I deserve to have for my trouble." The farmer was a sad miser, and knew that his man was very simple-hearted; so he took out threepence, and gave him for every year's service a penny. The poor fellow thought it was a great deal of money to have, and said to himself, "Why should I work hard, and live here on bad fare any longer? I can now travel into the wide world, and make myself merry." With that he put his money into his purse, and set out, roaming over hill and valley.

As he jogged along over the fields, singing and dancing, a little dwarf met him, and asked him what made him so merry. "Why, what should make me down-hearted?" said he; "I am sound in health and rich in purse, what should I care for? I have saved up my three years' earnings and have it all safe in my pocket." "How much may it come to?" said the little man. "Full threepence," replied the countryman. "I wish you would give them to me," said the other; "I am very poor." Then the man pitied him, and gave him all he had; and the little dwarf said in return, "As you have such a kind honest heart, I will grant you three wishes—one for every penny; so choose whatever you like." Then the countryman rejoiced at his good luck, and said, "I like many things better than money: first, I will have a bow that will bring down every thing I shoot at; secondly, a fiddle that will set every one dancing that hears me play upon it; and thirdly, I should like that every one should grant what I ask." The dwarf said he should have his three wishes; so he gave him the bow and fiddle, and went his way.

Our honest friend journeyed on his way too; and if he was merry before, he was now ten times more so. He had not gone far before he met an old miser: close by them stood a tree, and on the topmost twig sat a thrush singing away most joyfully. "Oh, what a pretty bird!" said the miser; "I would give a great deal of money to have such a one." "If that's all," said the countryman, "I will soon bring it down." Then he took up his bow, and down fell the thrush into the bushes at the foot of the tree. The miser crept into the bush to find it; but directly he had got into the middle, his companion took up his fiddle and played away, and the miser began to dance and spring about, capering higher and higher in the air. The thorns soon began to tear his clothes till they all hung in rags about him, and he himself was all scratched and wounded, so that the blood ran down. "Oh, for heaven's sake!" cried the miser, "master! master! pray let the fiddle alone. What have I done to deserve this?" "Thou hast shaved many a poor soul close enough," said the other; "thou art only meeting thy reward:" so he played up another tune. Then the miser began to beg and promise, and offered money for his liberty; but he did not come up to the musician's price for some time, and he danced him along brisker and brisker, and the miser bid higher and higher, till at last he offered a round hundred of florins that he had in his purse, and had just gained by cheating some poor fellow. When the countryman saw so much money, he said, "I will agree to your proposal." So he took the purse, put up his fiddle, and travelled on very well pleased with his bargain.

Meanwhile the miser crept out of the bush half-naked and in a piteous plight, and began to ponder how he should take his revenge, and serve his late companion some trick. At last he went to the judge, and complained that a rascal had robbed him of his money, and beaten him into the bargain; and that the fellow who did it carried a bow at his back and a fiddle hung round his neck. Then the judge sent out his officers to bring up the accused wherever they should find him; and he was soon caught and brought up to be tried.

The miser began to tell his tale, and said he had been robbed of his money. "No, you gave it me for playing a tune to you," said the countryman; but the judge told him that was not likely, and cut the matter short by ordering him off to the gallows.

So away he was taken; but as he stood on the steps he said, "My Lord Judge, grant me one last request." "Any thing but thy life," replied the other. "No," said he, "I do not ask my life; only to let me play upon my fiddle for the last time." The miser cried out, "Oh, no!

no! for heaven's sake don't listen to him! don't listen to him!" But the judge said, "It is only this once, he will soon have done." The fact was, he could not refuse the request, on account of the dwarf's third gift.

Then the miser said, "Bind me fast, bind me fast, for pity's sake." But the countryman seized his fiddle, and struck up a tune, and at the first note judge, clerks, and jailer were in motion; all began capering, and no one could hold the miser. At the second note the hangman let his prisoner go, and danced also, and by the time he had played the first bar of the tune, all were dancing together—judge, court, and miser, and all the people who had followed to look on. At first the thing was merry and pleasant enough; but when it had gone on a while, and there seemed to be no end of playing or dancing, they began to cry out, and beg him to leave off; but he stopt not a whit the more for their entreaties, till the judge not only gave him his life, but promised to return him the hundred florins.

Then he called to the miser, and said, "Tell us now, you vagabond, where you got that gold, or I shall play on for your amusement only." "I stole it," said the miser in the presence of all the people; "I acknowledge that I stole it and that you earned it fairly." Then the countryman stopt his fiddle, and left the miser to take his place at the gallows.

# THE LADY AND THE LION

A merchant, who had three daughters, was once setting out upon a journey; but before he went he asked each daughter what gift he should bring back for her. The eldest wished for pearls; the second for jewels; but the third said, "Dear father, bring me a rose." Now it was no easy task to find a rose, for it was the middle of winter; yet, as she was the fairest daughter, and was very fond of flowers, her father said he would try what he could do. So he kissed all three, and bid them good-bye. And when the time came for his return, he had bought pearls and jewels for the two eldest, but he had sought every where in vain for the rose; and when he went into any garden and inquired for such a thing, the people laughed at him, and asked him whether he thought roses grew in snow. This grieved him very much, for his third daughter was his dearest child; and as he was journeying home, thinking what he should bring her, he came to a fine castle; and around the castle was a garden, in half of which it appeared to be summer time, and in the other half winter. On one side the finest flowers were in full bloom, and on the other every thing looked desolate and buried in snow. "A lucky hit!" said he as he called to his servant, and told him to go to a beautiful bed of roses that was there, and bring him away one of the flowers. This done, they were riding away well pleased, when a fierce lion sprang up, and roared out, "Whoever dares to steal my roses shall be eaten up alive." Then the man said, "I knew not that the garden belonged to you;

can nothing save my life?" "No!" said the lion, "nothing, unless you promise to give me whatever meets you first on your return home; if you agree to this, I will give you your life, and the rose too for your daughter." But the man was unwilling to do so, and said, "It may be my youngest daughter, who loves me most, and always runs to meet me when I go home." Then the servant was greatly frightened, and said, "It may perhaps be only a cat or a dog." And at last the man yielded with a heavy heart, and took the rose; and promised the lion whatever should meet him first on his return.

And as he came near home, it was his youngest and dearest daughter that met him; she came running and kissed him, and welcomed him home; and when she saw that he had brought her the rose, she rejoiced still more. But her father began to be very melancholy, and to weep, saying, "Alas! my dearest child! I have bought this flower dear, for I have promised to give you to a wild lion, and when he has you, he will tear you in pieces, and eat you." And he told her all that had happened; and said she should not go, let what would happen.

But she comforted him, and said, "Dear father, what you have promised must be fulfilled; I will go to the lion, and soothe him, that he may let me return again safe home."

The next morning she asked the way she was to go, and took leave of her father, and went forth with a bold heart into the wood. But the lion was an enchanted prince, and by day he and all his court were lions, but in the evening they took their proper forms again. And when the lady came to the castle, he welcomed her so courteously that she consented to marry him.

118

The wedding-feast was held, and they lived happily together a long time. The prince was only to be seen as soon as evening came, and then he held his court; but every morning he left his bride, and went away by himself, she knew not whither, till night came again.

After some time he said to her, "To-morrow there will be a great feast in your father's house, for your eldest sister is to be married; and, if you wish to go to visit her, my lions shall lead you thither." Then she rejoiced much at the thoughts of seeing her father once more, and set out with the lions; and every one was overjoyed to see her, for they had thought her dead long since. But she told them how happy she was; and stayed till the feast was over, and then went back to the wood.

Her second sister was soon after married; and when she was invited to the wedding, she said to the prince, "I will not go alone this time; you must go with me." But he would not, and said that would be a very hazardous thing, for if the least ray of the torch light should fall upon him, his enchantment would become still worse, for he should be changed into a dove, and be obliged to wander about the world for seven long years. However, she gave him no rest, and said she would take care no light should fall upon him. So at last they set out together, and took with them their little child too; and she chose a large hall with thick walls, for him to sit in while the wedding torches were lighted; but unluckily no one observed that there was a crack in the door. Then the wedding was held with great pomp; but as the train came from the church, and passed with the torches before the hall, a very small ray of light fell upon the prince. In a moment he disappeared; and when his wife came in, and sought him, she found only a white dove. Then he said to her, "Seven years must I fly up and down over the face of the earth; but every now and then I will let fall a white feather, that shall show you the way I am going; follow it, and at last you may overtake and set me free."

This said, he flew out at the door, and she followed; and every now and then a white feather fell, and showed her the way she was to journey. Thus she went roving on through the wide world, and looked neither to the right hand nor to the left, nor took any rest for seven years. Then she began to rejoice, and thought to herself that the time was fast coming when all her troubles should cease; yet repose was still far off: for one day as she was travelling on, she missed the white feather, and when she lifted up her eyes she could no where see the dove. "Now," thought she to herself, "no human aid can be of use to me;" so she went to the sun, and said, "Thou shinest every where, on the mountain's top, and the valley's depth; hast thou any where seen a white dove?" "No," said the sun, "I have not seen it; but I will give thee a casket—open it when thy hour of need comes." So she thanked the sun, and went on her way till eventide; and when the moon arose, she cried unto it, and said, "Thou shinest through all the night, over field and grove: hast thou no where seen a white dove?" "No," said the moon, "I cannot help thee; but I will give thee an egg—break it when need comes." Then she thanked the moon, and went on till the night-wind blew; and she raised up her voice to it, and said, "Thou blowest through every tree and under every leaf: hast thou not seen the white dove?" "No," said the night-wind; "but I will ask three other winds; perhaps they have seen it." Then the east wind and the west wind came, and said they too had not seen it; but the south wind said, "I have seen the white dove; he has fled to the Red Sea, and is changed once more into a lion, for the seven years are passed away; and there he is fighting with a dragon, and the dragon is an enchanted princess, who seeks to separate him from you." Then the night-wind said, "I will give thee counsel: go to the Red Sea; on the right shore stand many rods; number them, and when thou comest to the eleventh, break it off and smite the dragon with it; so the lion will have the victory, and both of them will appear to you in their human forms. Then instantly set out with thy beloved prince, and journey home over sea and land."

So our poor wanderer went forth, and found all as the night-wind had said; and she plucked the eleventh rod, and smote the dragon, and immediately the lion became a prince and the dragon a princess again. But she forgot the counsel which the night-wind had given; and the false princess watched her opportunity, and took the prince by the arm, and carried him away.

Thus the unfortunate traveller was again forsaken and forlorn; but she took courage and said, "As far as the wind blows, and so long as the cock crows, I will journey on till I find him once again." She went on for a long way, till at length she came to the castle whither the princess had carried the prince; and there was a feast prepared, and she heard that the wedding was about to be held. "Heaven aid me now!" said she; and she took the casket that the sun had given her, and found that within it lay a dress as dazzling as the sun itself. So she put it on, and went into the palace; and all the people gazed upon her; and the dress pleased the bride so much that she asked whether it was to be sold: "Not for gold and silver," answered she; "but for flesh and blood." The princess asked what she meant; and she said, "Let me speak with the bridegroom this night in his chamber, and I will give thee the dress." At last the princess agreed; but she told her chamberlain to give the prince a sleeping-draught, that he might not hear or see her. When evening came, and the prince had fallen asleep, she was led into his chamber, and she sat herself down at his feet and said, "I have followed thee seven years; I have been to the sun, the moon, and the night-wind, to seek thee; and at last I have helped thee to overcome the dragon. Wilt thou then forget me quite?" But the prince slept so soundly that her voice only passed over him, and seemed like the murmuring of the wind among the fir-trees.

Then she was led away, and forced to give up the golden dress; and when she saw that there was no help for her, she went out into a meadow and sat herself down and wept. But as she sat she bethought herself of the egg that the moon had given her; and when she broke it, there ran out a hen and twelve chickens of pure gold, that played about, and then nestled under the old one's wings, so as to form the most beautiful sight in the world. And she rose up, and drove them before her till the bride saw them from her window, and was so pleased that she came forth, and asked her if she would sell the brood. "Not for gold or silver; but for flesh and blood: let me again this evening speak with the bridegroom in his chamber."

Then the princess thought to betray her as before, and agreed to what she asked; but when the prince went to his chamber, he asked the chamberlain why the wind had murmured so in the night. And the chamberlain told him all; how he had given him a sleeping-draught, and a poor maiden had come and spoken to him in his chamber, and was to come again that night. Then the prince took care to throw away the sleeping-draught; and when she came and began again to tell him what woes had befallen her, and how faithful and true to him she had been, he knew his beloved wife's voice, and sprung up, and said, "You have awakened me as from a dream; for the strange princess had thrown a spell around me, so that I had altogether forgotten you: but heaven hath sent you to me in a lucky hour."

And they stole away out of the palace by night secretly (for they feared the princess), and journeyed home; and there they found their child, now grown comely and fair, and lived happily together to the end of their days.

## OLD SULTAN

A shepherd had a faithful dog, called Sultan, who was grown very old, and had lost all his teeth. And one day when the shepherd and his wife were standing together before the house, the shepherd said, "I will shoot old Sultan to-morrow morning, for he is of no use now." But his wife said, "Pray let the poor faithful creature live; he has served us well a great many years, and we ought to give him a livelihood for the rest of his days." "But what can we do with him?" said the shepherd, "he has not a tooth in his head, and the thieves don't care for him at all; to be sure he has served us, but then he did it to earn his livelihood; to-morrow shall be his last day, depend upon it."

Poor Sultan, who was lying close by them, heard all that the shepherd and his wife said to one another, and was very much frightened to think to-morrow would be his last day; so in the evening he went to his good friend the wolf, who lived in the wood, and told him all his sorrows, and how his master meant to kill him in the morning. "Make yourself easy," said the wolf, "I will give you some good advice. Your master, you know, goes out every morning very early with his wife into the field; and they take their little child with them, and lay it down behind the hedge in the shade while they are at work. Now do you lie down close by the child, and pretend to be watching it, and I will come out of the wood and run away with it: you must run after me as fast as you can, and I will let it drop; then you may carry it back, and they will think you have saved their child, and will be so thankful to you that they will take care of you as long as you live." The dog liked this plan very well; and accordingly so it was managed. The wolf ran with the child a little way; the shepherd and his wife screamed out; but Sultan soon overtook him, and carried the poor little thing back to his master and mistress. Then the shepherd patted him on the head, and said, "Old Sultan has saved our child from the wolf, and therefore he shall live and be well taken care of, and have plenty to eat. Wife, go home, and give him a good dinner, and let him have my old cushion to sleep on as long as he lives." So from this time forward Sultan had all that he could wish for.

Soon afterwards the wolf came and wished him joy, and said, "Now, my good fellow, you must tell no tales, but turn your head the other way when I want to taste one of the old shepherd's fine fat sheep." "No," said

Sultan; "I will be true to my master." However, the wolf thought he was in joke, and came one night to get a dainty morsel. But Sultan had told his master what the wolf meant to do; so he laid wait for him behind the barn-door, and when the wolf was busy looking out for a good fat sheep, he had a stout cudgel laid about his back, that combed his locks for him finely.

Then the wolf was very angry, and called Sultan "an old rogue", and swore he would have his revenge. So the next morning the wolf sent the boar to challenge Sultan to come into the wood to fight the matter out. Now Sultan had no body he could ask to be his second but the shepherd's old three-legged cat; so he took her with him, and as the poor thing limped along with some trouble, she stuck up her tail straight in the air.

The wolf and the wild boar were first on the ground; and when they espied their enemies coming, and saw the cat's long tail standing straight in the air, they thought she was carrying a sword for Sultan to fight with; and every time she limped, they thought she was picking up a stone to throw at them; so they said they should not like this way of fighting, and the boar lay down behind a bush, and the wolf jumped up into a tree. Sultan and the cat soon came up, and looked about, and wondered that no one was there. The boar, however, had not quite hidden himself, for his ears stuck out of the bush; and when he shook one of them a little, the cat, seeing something move, and thinking it was a mouse, sprang upon it, and bit and scratched it, so that the boar jumped up and grunted, and ran away, roaring out, "Look up in the tree, there sits the one who is to blame." So they looked up, and espied the wolf sitting amongst the branches; and they called him a cowardly rascal, and would not suffer him to come down till he was heartily ashamed of himself, and had promised to be good friends again with old Sultan.

# THE TURNIP

There were two brothers who were both soldiers; the one was rich and the other poor. The poor man thought he would try to better himself; so, pulling off his red coat, he became a gardener, and dug his ground well, and sowed turnips.

When the seed came up, there was one plant bigger than all the rest; and it kept getting larger and larger, and seemed as if it would never cease growing; so that it might have been called the prince of turnips for there never was such a one seen before, and never will again. At last it was so big that it filled a cart, and two oxen could hardly draw it; and the gardener knew not what in the world to do with it, nor whether it would be a blessing or a curse to him. One day he said to himself, "What shall I do with it? if I sell it, it will bring no more than another; and for eating, the little turnips are better than this; the best thing perhaps is to carry it and give it to the king as a mark of respect."

Then he yoked his oxen, and drew the turnip to the Court, and gave it to the king. "What a wonderful thing!" said the king; "I have seen many strange things, but such a monster as this I never saw. Where did you get the seed? or is it only your good luck? If so, you are a true child of fortune." "Ah, no!" answered the gardener, "I am no child of fortune; I am a poor soldier, who never could get enough to live upon; so I laid aside my red coat, and set to work, tilling the ground. I have a brother, who is rich, and your majesty knows him well, and all the world knows him; but because I am poor, every body forgets me."

The king then took pity on him, and said, "You shall be poor no longer. I will give you so much that you shall be even richer than your brother." Then he gave him gold and lands and flocks, and made him so rich that his brother's fortune could not at all be compared with his.

When the brother heard of all this, and how a turnip had made the gardener so rich, he envied him sorely, and bethought himself how he could contrive to get the same good fortune for himself. However, he determined to manage more cleverly than his brother, and got together a rich present of gold and fine horses for the king; and thought he must have a much larger gift in return: for if his brother had received so much for only a turnip, what must his present be worth?

The king took the gift very graciously, and said he knew not what to give in return more valuable and wonderful than the great turnip; so the soldier was forced to put it into a cart, and drag it home with him. When he reached home, he knew not upon whom to vent his rage and spite; and at length wicked thoughts came into his head, and he resolved to kill his brother.

So he hired some villains to murder him; and having shown them where to lie in ambush, he went to his brother, and said, "Dear brother, I have found a hidden treasure; let us go and dig it up, and share it between us." The other had no suspicions of his roguery: so they went out together, and as they were travelling along, the murderers rushed out upon him, bound him, and were going to hang him on a tree.

But whilst they were getting all ready, they heard the trampling of a horse at a distance, which so frightened them that they pushed their prisoner neck and shoulders together into a sack, and swung him up by a cord to the tree, where they left him dangling, and ran away. Meantime he worked and worked away, till he made a hole large enough to put out his head.

When the horseman came up, he proved to be a student, a merry fellow, who was journeying along on his nag, and singing as he went. As soon as the man in the sack saw him passing under the tree, he cried out, "Good morning! good morning to thee, my friend!" The student looked about every where; and seeing no one, and not knowing where the voice came from, cried out, "Who calls me?"

Then the man in the tree answered, "Lift up thine eyes, for behold here I sit in the sack of wisdom; here have I, in a short time, learned great and wondrous things. Compared to this seat, all the learning of the schools is as empty air. A little longer, and I shall know all that man can know, and shall come forth wiser than the wisest of mankind. Here I discern the signs and motions of the heavens and the stars; the laws that control the winds; the number of the sands on the sea-shore; the healing of the sick; the virtues of all simples, of birds, and of precious stones. Wert thou but once here, my friend, thou wouldst feel and own the power of knowledge."

The student listened to all this and wondered much; at last he said, "Blessed be the day and hour when I found you; cannot you contrive to let me into the sack for a little while?" Then the other answered, as if very unwillingly,."A little space I may allow thee to sit here, if thou wilt reward me well and entreat me kindly; but thou must tarry yet an hour below, till I have learnt some little matters that are yet unknown to me."

So the student sat himself down and waited a while; but the time hung heavy upon him, and he begged earnestly that he might ascend forthwith, for his thirst of knowledge was great. Then the other pretended to give way, and said, "Thou must let the sack of wisdom descend, by untying yonder cord, and then thou shalt enter." So the student let him down, opened the sack, and set him free. "Now then," cried he, "let me ascend quickly." As he began to put himself into the sack heels first, "Wait a while," said the gardener, "that is not the way." Then he pushed him in head first, tied up the sack, and soon swung up the searcher after wisdom dangling in the air. "How is it with thee, friend?" said he, "dost thou not feel that wisdom comes unto thee? Rest there in peace, till thou art a wiser man than thou wert."

So saying, he trotted off on the student's nag, and left the poor fellow to gather wisdom till somebody should come and let him down.

# MRS FOX

There was once a sly old fox with nine tails, who was very curious to know whether his wife was true to him: so he stretched himself out under a bench, and pretended to be as dead as a mouse.

Then Mrs Fox went up into her own room and locked the door: but her maid, the cat, sat at the kitchen fire cooking; and soon after it became known that the old fox was dead, some one knocked at the door, saying,

"Miss Pussy! Miss Pussy! how fare you today?
Are you sleeping or watching the time away?"

Then the cat went and opened the door, and there stood a young fox; so she said to him,

"No, no, Master Fox, I don't sleep in the day,
I'm making some capital white wine whey.
Will your honour be pleased to dinner to stay?"

"No, I thank you," said the fox; "but how is poor Mrs Fox?" Then the cat answered,

"She sits all alone in her chamber up stairs,
And bewails her misfortune with floods of tears:
She weeps till her beautiful eyes are red;
For, alas! alas! Mr Fox is dead."

"Go to her," said the other, "and say that there is a young fox come, who wishes to marry her."

Then up went the cat,—trippety trap,
And knocked at the door,—tippety tap;
"Is good Mrs Fox within?" said she.
"Alas! my dear, what want you with me?"
"There waits a suitor below at the gate."

Then said Mrs Fox,

"How looks he, my dear? is he tall and straight?
Has he nine good tails? There must be nine,
Or he never shall be a suitor of mine."

"Ah!" said the cat, "he has but one." "Then I will
never have him," answered Mrs Fox.

So the cat went down, and sent this suitor about his
business. Soon after, some one else knocked at the door;
it was another fox that had two tails, but he was not
better welcomed than the first. After this came several
others, till at last one came that had really nine tails just
like the old fox.

When the widow heard this, she jumped up and
said,

"Now, Pussy, my dear, open windows and doors,
And bid all our friends at our wedding to meet;
And as for that nasty old master of ours,
Throw him out of the window, Puss, into the street."

But when the wedding feast was all ready, up sprung
the old gentleman on a sudden, and taking a club,
drove the whole company, together with Mrs Fox, out
of doors.

*

After some time, however, the old fox really died;
and soon afterwards a wolf came to pay his respects,
and knocked at the door.

*Wolf.* "Good day, Mrs Cat, with your whiskers so trim;
How comes it you're sitting alone so prim?
What's that you are cooking so nicely, I pray?"
*Cat.* "O, that's bread and milk for my dinner today.
Will your worship be pleased to stay and dine,
Or shall I fetch you a glass of wine?"

"No, I thank you! Mrs Fox is not at home, I suppose?"

*Cat.* "She sits all alone,
　Her griefs to bemoan;
　For, alas! alas! Mr Fox is gone."
*Wolf.* "Ah! dear Mrs Puss! that's a loss indeed:
　D'ye think she'd take *me* for a husband instead?"
*Cat.* "Indeed, Mr Wolf, I don't know but she may
　If you'll sit down a moment, I'll step up and see."
　So she gave him a chair, and shaking her ears,
　She very obligingly tripped it up stairs.
　She knocked at the door with the rings on her toes,
　And said, "Mrs Fox, you're within, I suppose?"
　"O yes," said the widow, "pray come in, my dear,
　And tell me whose voice in the kitchen I hear."
　"It's a wolf," said the cat, "with a nice smooth skin,
　Who was passing this way, and just stepped in
　To see (as old Mr Fox is dead)
　If you like to take him for a husband instead."

"But," said Mrs Fox, "has he red feet and a sharp snout?" "No," said the cat. "Then he won't do for me."
Soon after the wolf was sent about his business, there came a dog, then a goat, and after that a bear, a lion,

and all the beasts, one after another. But they all wanted
something that old Mr Fox had, and the cat was ordered
to send them all away. At last came a young fox, and
Mrs Fox said, "Has he four red feet and a sharp snout?"
"Yes," said the cat.

"Then, Puss, make the parlour look clean and neat,
And throw the old gentleman into the street;
A stupid old rascal! I'm glad that he's dead,
Now I've got such a charming young fox instead."
So the wedding was held, and the merry bells rung,
And the friends and relations they danced and they
     sung,
And feasted and drank, I can't tell how long.

## THE GIANT WITH THE
## THREE GOLDEN HAIRS

There was once a poor man who had an only son born
to him. The child was born under a lucky star; and those
who told his fortune said that in his fourteenth year he
would marry the king's daughter. It so happened that
the king of that land soon after the child's birth passed
through the village in disguise, and asked whether there
was any news. "Yes," said the people, "a child has just
been born, that they say is to be a lucky one, and when
he is fourteen years old, he is fated to marry the king's
daughter." This did not please the king; so he went
to the poor child's parents and asked them whether
they would sell him their son? "No," said they; but
the stranger begged very hard and offered a great deal

of money, and they had scarcely bread to eat, so at last they consented, thinking to themselves, he is a luck's child, he can come to no harm.

The king took the child, put it into a box, and rode away; but when he came to a deep stream, he threw it into the current, and said to himself, "That young gentleman will never be my daughter's husband." The box however floated down the stream; some kind spirit watched over it so that no water reached the child, and at last about two miles from the king's capital it stopt at the dam of a mill. The miller soon saw it, and took a long pole, and drew it towards the shore, and finding it heavy, thought there was gold inside; but when he opened it, he found a pretty little boy, that smiled upon him merrily. Now the miller and his wife had no children, and therefore rejoiced to see their prize, saying, "Heaven has sent it to us;" so they treated it very kindly, and brought it up with such care that every one admired and loved it.

About thirteen years passed over their heads, when the king came by accident to the mill, and asked the miller if that was his son. "No," said he, "I found him when a babe in a box in the mill-dam." "How long ago?" asked the king. "Some thirteen years," replied the miller. "He is a fine fellow," said the king, "can you spare him to carry a letter to the queen? it will please me very much, and I will give him two pieces of gold for his trouble." "As your majesty pleases," answered the miller.

Now the king had soon guessed that this was the child whom he had tried to drown; and he wrote a letter by him to the queen, saying, "As soon as the bearer of this arrives let him be killed and immediately buried, so that all may be over before I return."

The young man set out with this letter, but missed his way, and came in the evening to a dark wood. Through the gloom he perceived a light at a distance, towards which he directed his course, and found that it proceeded from a little cottage. There was no one within except an old woman, who was frightened at seeing him, and said, "Why do you come hither, and whither are you going?" "I am going to the queen, to whom I was to have delivered a letter; but I have lost my way, and shall be glad if you will give me a night's rest." "You are very unlucky," said she, "for this is a robbers' hut, and if the band returns while you are do here it may be worse for you." "I am so tired, however," replied he, "that I must take my chance, for I can go no farther;" so he laid the letter on the table, stretched himself out upon a bench, and fell asleep.

When the robbers came home and saw him, they asked the old woman who the strange lad was. "I have given him shelter for charity," said she; "he had a letter to carry to the queen, and lost his way." The robbers took up the letter, broke it open and read the directions which it contained to murder the bearer. Then their leader tore it, and wrote a fresh one desiring the queen, as soon as the young man arrived, to marry him to the king's daughter. Meantime they let him sleep on till morning broke, and then showed him the right way to the queen's palace; where, as soon as she had read the letter, she had all possible preparations made for the wedding; and as the young man was very beautiful, the princess took him willingly for her husband.

After a while the king returned; and when he saw the prediction fulfilled, and that this child of fortune was, notwithstanding all his cunning, married to his daughter, he inquired eagerly how this had happened, and what were the orders which he had given. "Dear husband," said the queen, "here is your letter, read it for yourself." The king took it, and seeing that an exchange had been made, asked his son-in-law what he had done with the letter which he had given him to carry. "I know nothing of it," answered he; "it must have been taken away in the night while I slept." Then the king was very wroth, and said, "No man shall have my daughter who does not descend into the wonderful cave and bring me three golden hairs from the head of the giant king who reigns there; do this and you shall have my consent." "I will soon manage that," said the youth;—so he took leave of his wife and set out on his journey.

At the first city that he came to, the guard of the gate stopt him, and asked what trade he followed and what he knew. "I know every thing," said he. "If that be so," replied they, "you are just the man we want; be so good as to tell us why our fountain in the market-place is dry and will give no water; find out the cause of that, and we will give you two asses loaded with gold." "With all my heart," said he, "when I come back."

Then he journeyed on and came to another city, and there the guard also asked him what trade he followed, and what he understood. "I know every thing," answered he. "Then pray do us a piece of service," said they, "tell us why a tree which used to bear us golden apples, now does not even produce a leaf." "Most willingly," answered he, "as I come back."

At last his way led him to the side of a great lake of water over which he must pass. The ferryman soon began to ask, as the others had done, what was his trade, and what he knew. "Every thing," said he. "Then," said the other, "pray inform me why I am bound for ever to ferry over this water, and have never been able to get my liberty; I will reward you handsomely." "I will tell you all about it," said the young man, "as I come home."

When he had passed the water, he came to the wonderful cave, which looked terribly black and gloomy. But the wizard king was not at home, and his grandmother sat at the door in her easy chair. "What do you seek?" said she. "Three golden hairs from the giant's head," answered he. "You run a great risk," said she, "when he returns home; yet I will try what I can do for you." Then she changed him into an ant, and told him to hide himself in the folds of her cloak. "Very well," said he: "but I want also to know why the city fountain is dry, why the tree that bore golden apples is now leafless, and what it is that binds the ferry-man to his post." "Those are three puzzling questions," said the old dame; "but lie quiet and listen to what the giant says when I pull the golden hairs."

Presently night set in and the old gentleman returned home. As soon as he entered he began to snuff up the air, and cried, "All is not right here: I smell man's flesh." Then he searched all round in vain, and the old dame scolded, and said, "Why should you turn every thing topsy-turvy? I have just set all in order." Upon this he laid his head in her lap and soon fell asleep. As soon as he began to snore, she seized one of the golden hairs and pulled it out. "Mercy!" cried he, starting up, "what are you about?" "I had a dream that disturbed me," said she, "and in my trouble I seized your hair: I dreamt that the fountain in the market-place of the city was become dry and would give no water; what can be the cause?"

"Ah! if they could find that out, they would be glad," said the giant: "under a stone in the fountain sits a toad; when they kill him, it will flow again."

This said, he fell asleep, and the old lady pulled out another hair. "What would you be at?" cried he in a rage. "Don't be angry," said she, "I did it in my sleep; I dreamt that in a great kingdom there was a beautiful tree that used to bear golden apples, and now has not even a leaf upon it; what is the reason of that?" "Aha!" said the giant, "they would like very well to know that secret: at the root of the tree a mouse is gnawing; if they were to kill him, the tree would bear golden apples again; if not, it will soon die. Now let me sleep in peace; if you wake me again, you shall rue it."

Then he fell once more asleep; and when she heard him snore she pulled out the third golden hair, and the giant jumped up and threatened her sorely; but she soothed him, and said, "It was a strange dream: methought I saw a ferryman who was fated to ply backwards and forwards over a lake, and could never be set at liberty; what is the charm that binds him?" "A silly fool!" said the giant; "if he were to give the rudder into the hand of any passenger, he would find himself at liberty, and the other would be obliged to take his place. Now let me sleep."

In the morning the giant arose and went out; and the old woman gave the young man the three golden hairs, reminded him of the answers to his three questions, and sent him on his way.

He soon came to the ferryman, who knew him again, and asked for the answer which he had promised him. "Ferry me over first," said he, "and then I will tell you." When the boat arrived on the other side, he told him to give the rudder to any of his passengers, and then he might run away as soon as he pleased. The next place he came to was the city where the barren tree stood: "Kill the mouse," said he, "that gnaws the root, and you will have golden apples again." They gave him a rich present, and he journeyed on to the city where the fountain had dried up, and the guard demanded his answer to their question. So he told them how to cure the mischief, and they thanked him and gave him the two asses laden with gold.

And now at last this child of fortune reached home. and his wife rejoiced greatly to see him, and to hear how well everything had gone with him. He gave the three golden hairs to the king, who could no longer raise any objection to him, and when he saw all the treasure, cried out in a transport of joy, "Dear son, where did you find all this gold?" "By the side of a lake," said the youth, "where there is plenty more to be had." "Pray, tell me," said the king, "that I may go and get some too." "As much as you please," replied the other; "you will see the ferryman on the lake, let him carry you across, and there you will see gold as plentiful as sand upon the shore."

Away went the greedy king; and when he came to the lake, he beckoned to the ferryman, who took him into his boat, and as soon as he was there gave the rudder into his hand, and sprung ashore, leaving the old king to ferry away as a reward for his sins.

"And is his majesty plying there to this day?" You may be sure of that, for nobody will trouble himself to take the rudder out of his hands.

# CHERRY, OR THE FROG-BRIDE

There was once a king who had three sons. Not far
from his kingdom lived an old woman who had an
only daughter called Cherry. The king sent his sons
out to see the world, that they might learn the ways
of foreign lands, and get wisdom and skill in ruling
the kingdom that they were one day to have for their
own. But the old woman lived at peace at home with
her daughter, who was called Cherry, because she liked
cherries better than any other kind of food, and would
eat scarcely any thing else. Now her poor old mother
had no garden, and no money to buy cherries every
day for her daughter; and at last there was no other
plan left but to go to a neighbouring nunnery-garden
and beg the finest she could get of the nuns; for she
dared not let her daughter go out by herself, as she was
very pretty, and she feared some mischance might befall
her. Cherry's taste was, however, very well known; and
as it happened that the abbess was as fond of cherries
as she was, it was soon found out where all the best
fruit went; and the holy mother was not a little angry
at missing some of her stock and finding whither it
had gone.

The princes while wandering on came one day to the
town where Cherry and her mother lived; and as they
passed along the street saw the fair maiden standing
at the window, combing her long and beautiful locks
of hair. Then each of the three fell deeply in love with
her, and began to say how much he longed to have her

for his wife! Scarcely had the wish been spoken, when all drew their swords, and a dreadful battle began; the fight lasted long, and their rage grew hotter and hotter, when at last the abbess hearing the uproar came to the gate. Finding that her neighbour was the cause, her old spite against her broke forth at once, and in her rage she wished Cherry turned into an ugly frog, and sitting in the water under the bridge at the world's end. No sooner said than done; and poor Cherry became a frog, and vanished out of their sight. The princes had now nothing to fight for; so sheathing their swords again, they shook hands as brothers, and went on towards their father's home.

The old king meanwhile found that he grew weak and ill-fitted for the business of reigning: so he thought of giving up his kingdom; but to whom should it be? This was a point that his fatherly heart could not settle; for he loved all his sons alike. "My dear children," said he, "I grow old and weak, and should like to give up my kingdom; but I cannot make up my mind which of you to choose for my heir, for I love you all three; and besides, I should wish to give my people the cleverest and best of you for their king. however, I will give you three trials, and the one who wins the prize shall have the kingdom. The first is to seek me out one hundred ells of cloth, so fine that I can draw it through my golden ring." The sons said they would do their best, and set out on the search.

The two eldest brothers took with them many followers, and coaches and horses of all sorts, to bring home all the beautiful clothes which they should find; but the youngest went alone by himself. They soon came to where the roads branched off into several ways; two

141

ran through smiling meadows, with smooth paths and shady groves, but the third looked dreary and dirty, and went over barren wastes. The two eldest chose the pleasant ways; and the youngest took his leave and whistled along over the dreary road. Whenever fine linen was to be seen, the two elder brothers bought it, and bought so much that their coaches and horses bent under their burthen. The youngest, on the other hand, journeyed on many a weary day, and found not a place where he could buy even one piece of cloth that was at all fine and good. His heart sunk beneath him, and every mile he grew more and more heavy and sorrowful. At last he came to a bridge over a stream, and there he sat himself down to rest and sigh over his bad luck, when an ugly-looking frog popped its head out of the water, and asked, with a voice that had not at all a harsh sound to his ears, what was the matter. The prince said in a pet, "Silly frog! thou canst not help me." "Who told you so?" said the frog; "tell me what ails you." After a while the prince opened the whole story, and told why his father had sent him out. "I will help you," said the frog; so it jumped back into the stream and soon came back dragging a small piece of linen not bigger than one's hand, and by no means the cleanest in the world in its look. However, there it was, and the prince was told to take it away with him. He had no great liking for such a dirty rag; but still there was something in the frog's speech that pleased him much, and he thought to himself, "It can do no harm, it is better than nothing;" so he picked it up, put it in his pocket, and thanked the frog, who dived down again, panting and quite tired, as it seemed, with its work. The farther he went the heavier he found to his great joy the pocket grow, and so he turned himself homewards, trusting greatly in his good luck.

He reached home nearly about the same time that his brothers came up, with their horses and coaches all heavily laden. Then the old king was very glad to see his children again, and pulled the ring off his finger to try who had done the best; but in all the stock which the two eldest had brought there was not one piece a tenth part of which would go through the ring. At this they were greatly abashed; for they had made a laugh of their brother, who came home, as they thought, empty-handed. But how great was their anger, when they saw him pull from his pocket a piece that for softness, beauty, and whiteness, was a thousand times better than any thing that was ever before seen! It was so fine that it passed with ease through the ring; indeed, two such pieces would readily have gone in together. The father embraced the lucky youth, told his servants to throw the coarse linen into the sea, and said to his children, "Now you must set about the second task which I am to set you;—bring me home a little dog, so small that it will lie in a nut-shell."

His sons were not a little frightened at such a task; but they all longed for the crown, and made up their minds to go and try their hands, and so after a few days they set out once more on their travels. At the cross-ways they parted as before, and the youngest chose his old dreary rugged road with all the bright hopes that his former good luck gave him. Scarcely had he sat himself down again at the bridge foot, when his old friend the frog jumped out, set itself beside him, and as before opened its big wide mouth, and croaked out, "What is the matter?" The prince had this time no doubt of the frog's power, and therefore told what he wanted. "It shall be done for you," said the frog; and springing into the stream it soon brought up a hazel-nut, laid it at his feet, and told him to take it home to his father, and crack it gently, and then see what would happen. The prince went his way very well pleased, and the frog, tired with its task, jumped back into the water.

His brothers had reached home first, and brought with them a great many very pretty little dogs. The old king, willing to help them all he could, sent for a large walnutshell and tried it with every one of the little dogs; but one stuck fast with the hind-foot out, and another with the head, and a third with the forefoot, and a fourth with its tail,—in short, some one way and some another; but none was at all likely to sit easily in this new kind of kennel. When all had been tried, the youngest made his father a dutiful bow, and gave him the hazel-nut, begging him to crack it very carefully: the moment this was done out ran a beautiful little white dog upon the king's hand, wagged its tail, fondled his new master, and soon turned about and barked at the other little beasts in the most graceful manner, to the delight of the whole court. The joy of every one was great; the old king again embraced his lucky son, told his people to drown all the other dogs in the sea, and said to his children, "Dear sons! your weightiest tasks are now over; listen to my last wish; whoever brings home the fairest lady shall be at once the heir to my crown."

The prize was so tempting and the chance so fair for all, that none made any doubts about setting to work, each in his own way, to try and be the winner. The youngest was not in such good spirits as he was the last time; he thought to himself, "The old frog has been able to do a great deal for me: but all its power must be nothing to me now, for where should it find me a fair maiden, still less a fairer maiden than was ever seen at my father's court? The swamps where it lives have no living things in them, but toads, snakes, and such vermin." Meantime he went on, and sighed as he sat down again with a heavy heart by the bridge. "Ah frog!" said he, "this time thou canst do me no good." "Never mind," croaked the frog: "only tell me what is the matter now." Then the prince told his old friend what trouble had now come upon him. "Go thy ways home," said the frog; "the fair maiden will follow hard after; but take care and do not laugh at whatever may happen!" This said, it sprang as before into the water and was soon out of sight. The prince still sighed on, for he trusted very little this time to the frog's word; but he had not set many steps towards home before he heard a noise behind him, and looking round saw six large water rats dragging along a large pumpkin like a coach, full trot. On the box sat an old fat toad as coachman, and behind stood two little frogs as footmen, and two fine mice with stately whiskers ran before as outriders; within sat his old friend the frog, rather misshapen and unseemly to be sure, but still with somewhat of a graceful air as it bowed to him in passing. Much too deeply wrapt in thought as to his chance of finding the fair lady whom he was seeking, to take any heed of the strange scene before him, the prince scarcely looked at it, and had still less mind to laugh. The coach passed on a little way, and soon turned a corner that hid it from his sight; but how astonished was he, on turning the corner himself, to find a handsome coach and six black horses standing

145

there, with a coachman in gay livery, and within, the most beautiful lady he had ever seen, whom he soon knew to be the fair Cherry, for whom his heart had so long ago panted! As he came up, the servants opened the coach door, and he was allowed to seat himself by the beautiful lady.

They soon came to his father's city, where his brothers also came, with trains of fair ladies; but as soon as Cherry was seen, all the court gave her with one voice the crown of beauty. The delighted father embraced his son, and named him the heir to his crown, and ordered all the other ladies to be thrown like the little dogs into the sea and drowned. Then the prince married Cherry, and lived long and happily with her, and indeed lives with her still—if he be not dead.